Lo

MW00945093

Jonathan Harnisch

Lover in the Nobody

Jonathan Harnisch

Babydude Press
36 Mariquita Lane
Corrales, New Mexico 87048
United States of America

While the publishers and the author have taken every care in preparing the material included in this work, any statements made as to the legal or other implications of any transaction, any particular method of litigation, or any kind of compensation claim are made in good faith purely for general guidance and cannot be regarded as a substitute for professional advice. Consequently, no liability can be accepted for loss or expense incurred as a result of relying on particular circumstances on statements made in this work.

Print Edition

British Library Cataloguing-in-Publication Data.

A catalogue record for this book is available from the British Library.

ISBN-13: 978-1505562460

ISBN-10: 1505562465

Library of Congress Control Number: 2014922575

CreateSpace Independent Publishing Platform, North Charleston, SC

Printed in the United States of America and Great Britain

First Edition

I wanted a complicated life.

— Jonathan Harnisch

Table of Contents

Georgie's Big Break

"Mr Gust?"

The secretary is standing over him. She waves her pencil in his face. "Mr Gust?"

Georgie looks up. He smiles at her. That's what people do, right? They smile?

She jerks the pencil toward the heavy wood door.

"The doctor's ready for you now," she says. She walks back to her desk, her tight little ass traveling smoothly in a clinging grey skirt. She props her yellow pumps up on the desk as she watches him. She grimaces and pulls out a nail file.

Georgie shuffles slowly over to the door, trying to keep his feet from lifting off the floor.

He leans over to open the door with his elbows, wanting to avoid the static shock he can feel rising in the roots of his hair; the electric charge traveling up his leg hair and his white, commercial-grade, psych-ward pants.

Then he realizes that sane people don't open doors with their elbows. Sane people just get shocked.

Georgie takes the shock with a snort and pushes the dark door open. Before him is Dr Abrams, a middle-aged man with salt-and-pepper hair.

"Good afternoon, Georgie," Dr Abrams says.

"Good afternoon, doc . . . Dr Abrams," Georgie replies.

Georgie raises his left foot and his right knee quivers. It's trying to hop, or something. He looks at the man seated behind the polished mahogany desk. With a silent growl, Georgie places his left foot on the floor. In front of the right. He sinks into the small leather chair and smiles tentatively.

"Well?" he says, daring the doc to say he is not cured. (Cured? Hah.)

"Well, Georgie. How are you feeling today?" Dr Abrams smiles right back, in that pseudo-friendly way he has.

"Great. Fantastic. I think I could walk right out of here today."

He stresses the word "walk."

The doc grins. "Well, there are good days and there are bad days, Georgie."

Georgie can see this is Dr Abrams' game, and he is not going to play it.

"I got a lot of good days ahead of me, doc. And I don't want to spend them in a nuthouse."

Dr Abrams sighs. "Georgie, you committed yourself. Six months ago, you knew that you had a problem. Now you've regressed. You're in denial, Georgie. Trust me, and the other physicians. You have a long way to go yet, Georgie. A long way "

"A g-great point, Dr Abrams," Georgie says. He curses himself for letting the stutter slip. On today of all days! But Georgie perseveres. "A great point—that I committed myself. If I committed myself, I can uncommit myself."

Dr Abrams shakes his head sadly.

"This is me, uncommitting myself," Georgie insists. "Look, I'm better. I walked in here without a hop. I haven't said a word about the voices. But do you know what? They're gone. Totally gone. And the Tourette's? Well, I'm stuck with that forever, but that's hardly a committable offense—"

Dr Abrams cuts him off.

"Georgie, to tell you the truth, your therapist gave me a call this morning."

(Dr C? Is it you?)

"I looked you up. Your family. And you are a high-ticket in here."

"What do you mean?" Georgie's first hint of fear is a tic in his right cheek. Not today! Georgie commands himself.

"I'd like to keep you in here," Dr Abrams concludes.

Georgie shrugs, playing it cool. "I'm outta here. I will walk right out of here."

"Against medical advice?" Dr Abrams rolls his eyes to the ceiling. He presses his fingertips together.

It's all an act, Georgie knows. All Dr Abrams needs is to know that Georgie is not bouncing off the walls, shredding his precious books, or ripping the leather from the chairs. . . . As long as Georgie doesn't do that, he can do whatever he wants. Except leave.

If they only knew what trouble their money was going to bring, Georgie thinks, my wretched parents would have thought twice.

He laughs.

No they wouldn't have.

"Georgie," Mr Abrams continues. "Georgie, you tried to kill yourself. For your personal safety, we have to keep you here until we are sure that you won't try to do it again."

This time that "friendly" smile is gone. Replaced with a smirk.

Georgie stares silently, not saying a word. He wants to stand, to shake Dr Abrams until his tonsils fall out on the floor, to throw him out the window, them jump out himself, and use the body as a cushion. Then steal Abram's car . . . . Georgie wonders if Abrams keeps his keys in his jacket pocket or somewhere in his desk.

No, stop it, Georgie thinks. Sane people don't think about that.

(Isn't that right, Dr C? I've always wondered.)

Dr Abrams sighs again.

"Okay, that's fine. You'll still have to wait for us to get your paperwork together."

Georgie's eyes light up. Then he sees something in the doc's face.

"How long will that take?" he asks.

"As long . . ." Dr Abrams' voice trails off, a funny glint coming into his eyes. "As long as it takes," he concludes.

Georgie screams, but there is no sound.

Dear Diary:

To worry is to waste time. Worrying doesn't change anything. It only robs one of his or her joy and peace of mind, simply keeping one busy doing absolutely nothing, when it comes down to it.

Georgie Gust Takes a Stand

Claudia, that bitch, whore, that woman I love and hate. (Who's Claudia?) She created a paradise and set it aflame. She is my world and its end, my kinky sex goddess, my creepy-crawly nemesis.

Remember her, in all her glory. Sleeping soundly under a teal-colored dream catcher in her red and white four-poster. She never stood a chance. I never stood a chance. We love and hate no matter whose face she's wearing, whose heart she's tearing.

I want to see her in those slingbacks, her perverted, cotton candy-blue toes peeking out to play.

But I won't. Not this time.

Georgie Gust loops and ties a thick piece of rope into a noose.

Not this time, not this time, not this time.

For Georgie, everything comes in threes. His stutters, his mutters, his women, his crazy step, step, hop. Everything.

(This time is different. This time, Ben controls my destiny. But this time, I end it all before any other bastard has a chance to end it for me, even Ben.)

He tosses the rope's looped end over the supporting beam in his old-world style, country living room. Then steps onto a chair and ties it tight. He cringes slightly, and lowers the loop over his head and tightens it around his neck.

He steps off the chair and kicks it away.

Georgie swings.

The rope burns his throat; he gurgles, trying to cough. His hands scrabble at his neck. His feet kick wildly, wanting to stand. Not this time.

Georgie Gust gasps, and a small trickle of air cools his throat. It's not enough. Not this time. Lightning bugs, fireworks burst behind his eyeballs. His whole body trembles and tingles and yells at him. He tries to scream again, this time emitting sound, but he cannot.

His heartbeat drums in his ears, pounding and pulsing with the blood in his eyeballs.

Thud . . . thud . . . thud.

Georgie moans, as the world turns black in his eyes.

Thud . . . thud . . . thud . . .

Dear Diary:

We're often asked, "How are you?" When I ask myself, and really think about it—good or bad—or in-between, it always seems to come down to the "overall" picture. Overall, I am well. Overall, I do my best. Overall, I am OK. Nothing's really black or white, but rather, overall. . .

Proof You Can Go Home Again

The black sedan pulls up to the curb outside Georgie Gust's old-style country home. The driver, Ben (Ben? Ben, again? The same Ben? You, Ben?) jumps out and runs to open the back door. Georgie pulls himself up out of the back seat.

(I thought Georgie was dead, Ben.

Well he is and he's not, Dr C. You know those creepy-crawly walking corpses—those dead but not-quite-dead people?

Like zombies, Ben?

Sure, sure. Like zombies, Dr C. If that's what helps you sleep at night.

Whatever you say, Ben. It's your story, now.)

Ben is at the trunk, pulling suitcases up and onto the sidewalk. Georgie pauses for a minute, looks at him. Then shrugs and walks up to his front door. His face is calm, peaceful. Not a tic in sight.

A brand new man, he thinks, his hand on the doorknob. Everything starts over now.

Thud . . . thud . . . thud.

A week later, a knock sounds on Georgie's front door.

He opens the door. It's Margaret, Georgie's only friend, as if he's ever had any actual friends, and true friends. He finds her annoying because she seems to care, but a tad too much, for whatever reason, though she does answer phone calls for a national crisis helpline, so it must simply be a part of her nature, to help the disenfranchised, desolate people who otherwise roam the world in their quiet introverted solitude.

Though surprised, he acts normal.

"I didn't call," he says.

"I know," Margaret says. Her perfect brown curls flood over her creamy skin. "I just wanted to see how things were going."

"Of course," he says. "Uh, come in. No, would you like to sit on the porch?"

She nods.

"Drink?"

She nods. "Water."

When Georgie comes out to the porch she is sitting comfortably on his dusty, handmade wicker chair.

"How've you been?" she begins. "I know it's only been a week, but . . . "

"Oh, great," Georgie says. He nods a little too enthusiastically. "Really. I'm like a new person." He smiles, his face a comfortable mask.

"I'm so glad to hear that," she gushes. "I had a really, really great time on the trip, you know. I can't believe it. Already, it's like a dream. We met the Dalai Lama! And trekked over the mountains. Do you remember that guy? With the chickens?" She sighs. "It was an amazing trip."

"Yeah. Amazing," Georgie nods. "The Dalai Lama. His spirit is so beautiful. Just being around him, everything felt easier, or something."

Margaret shines. "I'm so glad, Georgie, I just, you know when I found you, that day, when you were trying to . . ." Her voice fades at his blank stare.

"Well, I'm just so glad I found you. Just think, you couldn't have met the Dalai Lama if you were, well . . ." She shakes her head rapidly.

"Yeah, I know." He smiles sardonically. "Life is just great. Super."

"Yeah. Thank you, for thinking of me when your therapist recommended the trip."

Georgie shrugs. "Sure, the doc, you know, Dr C, she thought I should ask you." He doesn't say: Because you're the only person I know who actually seems to give a crap.

Margaret looks at him from the corner of her eye. She inhales, then pauses, opens her mouth.

"Georgie," she asks softly, "why did you do it?"

(You need a reason in this shitehole world?)

"I don't know. I . . ." He can't tell her about Claudia. Claudia hasn't happened yet.

He fixes on a memory.

"It was hard to grow up with Tourette's," he says quickly. "And my parents were sh-shitey, I mean, well, even now I don't ever see them. They weren't around when I was a kid, either. All I had was this nanny."

He pauses. Margaret glows at him, so proud of herself for having gotten him to open up.

(You think you can fix this?
Why not, Ben? Are you unfixable?
Whatever.)

Georgie stifles an overwhelming urge to laugh. He coughs instead.

"Go on," Margaret whispers.

"So, this nanny, she was horrible. Bad in every way. Like, she used to pinch me and uh, grab at me and stuff. You know, inappropriately?"

Margaret leans back and inhales through her teeth. "That's horrible!" she says.

"Yeah, they had to do surgeries and stuff. To uh, make me normal-looking."

Margaret looks at him inquisitively, not getting it.

"She used to hold me in the air, by my dick. Basically, nothing but . . ."

He trails off at her fierce blush.

(Is that even possible, Ben?

I get it, Dr C, it's yet another delusion, eh?)

One day, Georgie is going to learn when to speak and when to shut the hell up.

But today is not that day.

"So, I don't know. The doc says I'm all messed up about that," Georgie concludes lamely.

Margaret shifts in her seat. Georgie suddenly notices her toes, which she painted jungle-red for the trip to Tibet. The edges are chipped now—worn out from weeks of sandals and dirt roads, from chlorinated water and unadulterated sunlight.

"Well, I think you're so, so much better now."

She smiles warmly. Then she leans over and hugs him, awkwardly, since they are sitting in separate chairs. His brain whirrs at her smell.

Then she stands.

"Thank you so much for having me over, Georgie. And thanks for the trip. It was amazing."

She smiles down on him. The bright afternoon sunshine glows at the tips of her hair, making her face a blank mask. "I'm so glad that you're doing well." With that, she leaves.

Shortly thereafter, Georgie leaves, too.

Georgie might or might not be all better. He thinks to himself: *Maybe I am, and maybe I'm not. And either way, I certainly don't seem to care much.*

(See what I mean, Doc? It's the best indication of Georgie's sanity. Sane people do not go around wondering whether or not they are crazy. They just know they have nothing to worry about.

Lucky bastards.)

Georgie wanders through the kitchen, making himself a bowl of cereal.

But crazy people, Georgie thinks, crazy people are exactly the same way.

There's only that brief transition period, somewhere between sane and insane, where a person is truly able to fear that their mind has gone.

Georgie sits down in his dark living room for a moment, then glances at the window blinds. Fortunately brief, Georgie resists the urge to descend into a catatonic stare. But he doesn't ask himself why. Instead, he stands and decides to eat his cereal on the porch. Healthy people spend lots of time outside. In the light.

In the morning, Georgie shuffles slowly into the kitchen. The coffee machine is just burbling out the last ounce of coffee; its clock reads 10:00 am. Georgie glances at the refrigerator, and his magnetized eraser board that reads: "To Do List." Beneath the line, the board is blank.

Georgie pulls a clean mug from the cupboard and pours himself a cup of coffee. He moves over to the back door, admiring his beautifully landscaped backyard with the Italian cypress, the trimmed hedges. Such a contrast to the old-world, country-feel inside. He breathes in the aroma of the coffee then walks back through the kitchen, towards the front door.

From the corner of his eye, Georgie sees that the light on his answering machine blinks red. He stops, takes a slow sip of coffee, and presses the play button.

"Hi Georgie," Margaret's voice echoes from the machine. "It's Margaret. I was just thinking about what we talked about yesterday, remember? Anyway, this morning when I woke up, it occurred to me . . . Well, I thought it would be a good idea for you to maybe, maybe find your old nanny, you know?"

Georgie frowns as he stares at the machine.

"And you could confront her about everything she did to you and maybe get some closure or something? I don't know. Talk it over with your therapist maybe, but it came into my head like lightning."

Georgie's finger plunges toward the answering machine.

"Message deleted," the machine chimes. "You have no new messages."

Dear Diary:

It's not a sprint. It's a marathon.

Claudia Moves In (Part I)

Georgie moves out the front door, his coffee in hand. He pulls the mail from the mailbox and sits on the porch. He takes a sip and then sets the coffee mug down.

A woman's voice tickles his ear.

"Come here, little boy. Come here."

Georgie turns. The woman who stares at him is in her 40s, with wild-frizzy red hair.

"Hi," Georgie says.

"Hi, neighbor. I'm Claudia. I know we haven't met yet . . . but, well, I just moved in."

"Yeah? I hadn't realized." Her gaze entrances Georgie. Then he looks down.

Her bare feet. Her big pale feet. Her perfect, long, skinny toes. Her adolescent pink nail polish partially chipped off. She intoxicates him.

"Well, it's nice to meet you," Claudia says. He looks up at her, dizzy.

"Yeah . . . I'm Georgie."

"I'll see you later, Georgie," she says.

Later that week, Georgie goes to the grocery store. Now that he has met the Dalai Lama, now that he is a new man, he goes to the store once a week. Or so he says.

When he turns the corner, there she is. Margaret.

"Georgie!" she calls. There is no escaping. He stays put, lets her approach him.

"Georgie," she says again. "How have you been?"

"Great," he says, "Just great."

"Did you get my message?" Margaret asks. "The one . . . about your nanny?"

Georgie shifts uneasily. "Yeah, yeah," he says.

"What do you think? Did you try to find her?"

"Uh, no. Well, I'm going to, you know. But it's not easy. I was going to do it to-tomorrow."

Margaret beams.

"Oh, that's so wonderful Georgie! I'm so glad."

He nods, looking around him carefully. He fixates on a can of creamed corn.

"I just know it will help Georgie, I just know it," Margaret gushes.

"Y-yeah. Me, too," Georgie says unconvincingly. "Well, uh. Gotta go " . . . ."

He gestures to the end of the aisle, then shuffles toward it, engrossed in escape. Escape from Margaret and all she wants to say. He is so engrossed, he almost forgets to check out, and is reminded by the alarm that sounds when he strides toward the door.

"Damn it," Georgie mutters. He turns around and holds his basket high in the air. "Sorry. Sorry!" he announces, showing everyone that he is not a thief.

Somewhere, Margaret is watching him. Somewhere, Margaret has seen this almost occurrence of shoplifting. Somewhere, Margaret knows exactly how not fine Georgie really is.

Georgie sighs and stands in line with the rest of his fellow shoppers.

Later that day, Georgie walks up the front walk to his home, bags of groceries slung from his fists. On his front porch is an unexpected note:

Georgie Porgie,

Having not seen you in some time, my affection toward you has cooled to mere fondness. I'm becoming indifferent. I don't want that. We've been separated from each other far too often, though you live right next door. I want to see you again, Georgie. Tonight . . . .,

XXX

Claudia

Affection? What is this woman talking about?

Georgie wonders if they have met before, maybe in another lifetime he can't remember, maybe last week at a bar. But he can't think, can't think . . . .

Georgie's mind is stuck on repeat. His balls scream for release.

Claudia is a bombshell.

That night, Georgie abandons his bright new self and rushes over to Claudia's. It's there that the two are surrounded by vanilla-scented candlelight.

(Lust always wins over self-enlightenment. That's why we are at once so prolific and so infinitely ridiculous.)

Georgie wears a light blue dress shirt with a loose tie and ripped denims.

Claudia is completely naked.

"I can't believe you've never given a girl a pedicure," she purrs.

"Believe it. I'm a virgin, Claudia." Georgie is solemn.

She sits in the candle-lit bathroom, her plump cushion perched on her toilet bowl.

Georgie holds her foot in his lap. He is in agony, and enjoying every minute of it.

(Are we being sensual? Good God damn! You bet we are!)

Claudia hands over a bright red container of Tiger Balm. Georgie massages her feet with his eyes closed.

"Mmm. That's so relaxing. It tingles. It's warm," she moans.

He removes her old pink nail polish with store-brand nail polish remover.

"Well, aren't you the quick learner?" Claudia smiles.

Georgie fills a small footbath with a vanilla-scented soak. In five minutes, Claudia is asleep. He carefully removes her beautiful, clean, pasty-white feet from the warm water and pats them dry. He greases the palms of his hands with a hefty dose of rose-scented heel balm. Then he massages her feet from the toes down to her heels. Her feet twitch a little. She shivers.

By the time Georgie finishes, Claudia's feet are cotton-soft. He kisses them, hoping she will not wake up. A sad smile passes across her face. Is she dreaming? She is heavenly and peaceful. He can't stop staring.

Her eyes flash open.

"Well done. Well done, mister." She smiles. "How do you know so much about pedicures, if you've never done one before?"

Georgie blushes. "Well, I've seen . . . I've watched how they're done. At the sa-salon."

"Good boy," Claudia says.

Georgie buffs her toenails furiously, starting to have a little fun.

"What color would you like?" he asks.

"What do you think? What would look good on me?" Claudia looks him up and down meaningfully. "What would you choose, say, if you could have my toes?"

Georgie's groin stick straightens up as though by command. Pre-cum leaks into his denim crotch. He touches it for a second, a nano-second.

"What are you doing?" She busts him. She laughs.

"Nothing." Georgie pouts.

She pouts right back at him, raising her eyebrows.

He flinches away from her all-too-knowing gaze.

He carefully paints her nails, separating her toes with cotton balls. He colors them with two coats of "Hooker Blue." He paints them rapidly, sweating and breathing heavily. When he is finished, he stands and swivels, making his way to the doorway. He has to get out of there, back across the yard to his own peaceful sanctuary . . . that sterile environment where his cum is safe to splurge. He will splash it into the bathtub and wash it down with a shower, safe. Safe to fertilize the fishes and alligators and rats of the sewer.

"Neighbor, wait!" Claudia calls.

"Gotta go. Sorry."

"But now I'm too late for the party," she exclaims.

Georgie stops in his tracks.

"I want to congratulate you on what a great job you did on my pedicure! And on such short notice, too."

He smiles, horny as all hell.

"Now it's your turn."

Georgie's face gets that dreamy look.

"Sit down," she commands. Georgie seats himself on the toilet; she sits herself on the floor. Perfectly naked. Her shaved pussy smiles up at him coyly from the cold, white, sterile linoleum.

He wants to smell it.

"Take off your clothes," she commands.

Georgie attempts to undress slowly, but misses the mark completely. When he sits again, his boner stands at attention. Claudia tsks playfully.

"This has become your night, after all," she teases. "I need to thank you for the great job you've done, neighbor."

She stresses the word "job."

"Uh, well, thank you," Georgie says awkwardly.

"You like feet?" she asks respectfully.

Before Georgie can respond, her freshly pedicured feet creep up his thigh and begin to gently rub his balls and shaft. Georgie is queasy, sick, dizzy, in heaven, in agony. He can see right into her crotch. Her shaved pussy drips wet on the tile. Her vagina looks so lonely.

Within a minute, he can't take it any longer. He cries out in a strange squeal that makes her flinch slightly.

"Claudia, you've got to make me cum!" Georgie demands. "Fast. Please? Please?"

Her feet begin to stroke his erect cock up and down. It is tall, proud, rising toward his face. All his boiling love-sap about to explode.

"Do you want to cum in my mouth?" Claudia asks.

"On your feet. Just like that. Don't stop. Don't stop," he begs.

"Are you close?"

And, before he can answer, his white nut cascades over her toes.

Georgie wakes up on the cold tile of her bathroom floor early that morning. Claudia is sleeping, leaned up against the bathtub, her jaw slack. The light slanting in through the doorway shows every line of her face. She is old, but fertile. Her hair glows like flame.

Claudia represents flashes of a future, a world on fire. Georgie, seeking his lifelong orgasm, knows that she is trouble. But that's just what he needs—a world on fire.

Forget the Dalai Lama, that happy, self-sufficient self that Georgie has always known he could be. Fuck that shite.

He just wants Claudia, and all the joy/hate/love/torture/sex she promises.

Georgie leaves her place early, while she is still sleeping.

In his kitchen, he glances at the refrigerator door. The magnetized board still reads "To Do List," and nothing else.

He doesn't hear from her at all that day.

Or the following week.

He doesn't hear from her, but he sees her. Watches her, more like it. The side of the house that faces hers?—he lives on that side of the house now. Every movement from her yard sends him running for a window. He can't help himself. That wild hair, those purple-circled eyes, that feral laugh, those toes. Those toes.

He can't see her toes without using binoculars, so he keeps the binoculars right on the windowsill.

He is sick. He has a problem.

(You're telling me? Shite.)

Georgie hardly ever leaves his cage of paradise to enter the real world. Even though he feels pretty damn good lately, even though he is a new man.

(Yeah. Right. Exactly who does he think he's kidding?)

But sooner or later, he has to eat.

Georgie shuffles through the kitchen; his countertops and sink, cluttered with dirty dishes, soggy pizza boxes. He lifts his favorite mug. Sniffs it. Not too bad, he thinks. A little grungy around the edges. The coffee machine clock reads 2:02 pm. *Fuck the swill, man,* he commands himself, *just drink the shite.*

Georgie pours the coffee into his mug and wrinkles his nose. He stands and stares at the refrigerator door. The eraser board. His hand twitches.

Georgie pushes his cart through the grocery store. Every third step, he takes a small hop. Just a small one.

He turns the corner, and there she is again.

Margaret.

He would turn and escape, but he can't. Instead, his cart slams right into hers. They are tangled now, a mess of intertwining wires.

"Georgie!" she says.

He nods. Once, twice, three times.

"Georgie," she says again, "how are you?"

"G-great. J-just great."

She looks at him from the corner of her eye and backs away a little. "You sure, Georgie?" she whispers.

He coughs. Straightens up. "Yes," he says. "Of course."

"Did you get in touch with your nanny yet?"

"Uh, yeah. Well. I'm still tracking her down. I'll let you know."

Georgie looks down at his feet, at the shelves, at anything.

Margaret wrinkles her brow. "Yeah, I guess that would be hard."

"Yeah."

She waits, but he will not speak.

"Well, uh . . . I guess I'll catch you later, right?" she says finally.

"Yeah, yeah."

"Good to see you."

"Yeah."

Georgie shuffles into his kitchen and drops a single, lightweight grocery bag on the counter. He stares at the refrigerator, at the eraser board, at the to do list, which has "GET CIGARETTES" scrawled on it in thick pen. He lifts the pen and checks cigarettes off the list.

Georgie sits on the front porch, a lit cigarette dangling from his lips. Healthy people spend time outside, he thinks to himself. He inhales smoke deep, deep into his lungs. He feels the reassurance of the thick black stuff spread from his lungs outward.

He smiles, calmed.

Georgie is a bundle of purpose, a self-made man. Self-assuredly, he steps from task to task throughout the day. By the end of each day, he is exhausted, and pleased with his progress.

Oh, yes. Georgie is a man of energy, a man whose drive to succeed, to excel, is surpassed by very few.

Really.

It's a sunny day outside, but every blind is turned down inside Georgie's home, making it feel like one gigantic, single, dark shadow. As he wanders through each gloomy room, he eventually stops in the study, and glances down at his answering machine.

The light is flashing.

When did the phone ring? Georgie wonders. Why didn't I hear it?

He presses the play button.

"Hey, Georgie," a familiar voice echoes. "It's your mo—"

Georgie's finger jams down hard on the delete button.

"Message deleted," the machine informs him coldly.

Still, Georgie can hear his mother's voice echoing in his head: "You ungrateful bastard. You never appreciated a thing I ever did."

"You have no new messages," the machine chimes.

Georgie takes a cigarette out of his pack and puts it in his mouth. He doesn't light it. The cigarette dangles loosely from his lips as he walks over to the coffee pot—always on, never off; it is still half-full of old coffee. He fills a dirty coffee mug and takes a sip. The coffee's so hot it burns his tongue. Georgie drops the mug on the kitchen floor. Coffee spills everywhere as the mug shatters into countless pieces.

Georgie stares at the spilled coffee, the remains of the broken mug, and walks to the bathroom.

On the can, Georgie looks at the silver toilet paper dispenser. The roll is empty. His bleary, worn-out face is also blank, empty.

He steps into the shower, talking to himself.

The soap drops, thudding as it strikes the porcelain tub.

Georgie bends; he slips and falls.

"God damn," he moans.

What a way to start the day, eh?

Georgie tries to start anew in the kitchen. He lines up 10 espresso cups on the counter, each filled with black liquid tar. He pours sugar into each cup, running back and forth across the lineup, an unlit cigarette dangling from his lips.

Georgie pours each cup into a large thermos. He walks out of the kitchen, stepping right into the spilled coffee and porcelain shards. Coffee splashes up over his feet, but Georgie doesn't notice.

He walks into the living room, carrying the thermos. It doesn't look quite comfortable enough, so he opts for the porch; but something doesn't feel right there either. Sipping from his thermos, burning his tongue with espresso, Georgie stumbles through the house to his bedroom.

He collapses onto the blankets, groaning as his legs and back relax into the mattress. He props a pillow under his head and sips, sips, sips away at his black liquid tar.

After downing half the thermos, Georgie steps into the bathroom. He turns on the hot water in the shower and just lets it run. Steam fills the air and moistens his lungs.

Georgie needs something to satisfy him, to give him that everlasting orgasm he craves. Claudia is caput, now nothing but a ghost. She is out of the picture.

He walks into the house, a lightweight shopping bag spinning from his fingers. He erases the check mark next to "CIGARETTES" on his to do list and then rechecks it.

Dear Diary:

I need to finally forget about being impressive and commit to being real. Because being real is impressive!

Emptying His Pockets

On a desert highway, the midday sun reflects off the tinted windows of a moving stretch limousine; its pearl-white paint muddies with the billowing clouds in the sky.

Inside the limo, up front, a street map is open.

Our driver, Ben, focuses on the long, straight road ahead. He sniffs.

Georgie has a face full of self-help literature. A pair of trendy new shoes lies on the floor beside his socked feet. Georgie takes a long breath through his nose, closing the book that he has just finished. Its cover reads *Twelve Steps for Stupid People*.

"Why are you always reading those?" Ben asks.

Georgie's right eyelid flutters exactly nine times. Georgie knows. He counts. He likes to count.

"I like to see what will happen if I do the exact opposite," he says.

Ben nods. "That sounds reasonable."

They both pause, contemplating the anti-wisdom of self-help books. The desert rolls by, silently mocking.

(Mocking Ben? Really? It's just an ecosystem.

'Course, mocking. There's no bigger "fuck you" to a man like Georgie, a man living a sterile existence, than life as an ecosystem.

A man like Georgie, Ben? Or a man like you?

Let it go, Dr C.)

"Here we are," Ben finally says.

The limousine pulls up to the iron gates of a palatial mansion. A trio of security guards in uniform open the door for Georgie. Ben is directed to a smaller outbuilding around back.

On the hot, black asphalt just within the gates, Georgie strips to nothing. The desert swelters behind him, sending up wavering gusts of invisible heat. Georgie shuffles along carefully on the burning asphalt, keeping his head down.

He is quickly joined by staff members wearing psych attire—white shirts, black belts, white pants, and shoes. They are clean, sterile people—perfect for Georgie.

"This way," one says, his lips pale against the blanched cream of his skin. Georgie steps through the open door of the mansion and turns to the right.

The patio and interior are slate and marble, clean and cool. The floor is coated with naked people, all lying on their backs. Georgie meanders through them like a zombie, unsure of his place in the carpet of bodies. The house seems dead, but is somehow breathing. The rank scent of vinegar assails his nose.

Georgie finds a small space. He lies on the floor on his back, waiting. He shivers, slightly.

A loud siren screams and screeches and a horde of young, naked women flood the room and scatter. Rushing among the naked bodies, one by one they match themselves to pairs of feet. Georgie's woman is creamy-skinned, with wild, red, frizzy hair and a scarred lip. She grins, and her scar turns the smile to a grimace.

Georgie holds back a momentary panic.

As one, the women drop to the floor. Georgie's redhead rubs his toes a few times then sniffs his feet. She grins again—that same lopsided smile. This time, Georgie is able to relax. He is in a safe arena—he and she are nothing but strangers. Their nakedness means nothing. They are surrounded by wriggling, mewling grubs.

She strokes his ankles lightly, and his dick springs to attention. She grins her approval. Then swiftly she lowers herself over his toes. His eyes zoom in on her pink crotch. It quivers, glistening wet.

She pulls his toes inside of her. Georgie gasps, jerking slightly at the feel of her. Her wet flesh sucks at him as she imbeds his foot inside her slick pussy.

"Oh, God," Georgie moans. His eyes close in ecstasy.

Around him, similar noises rise as his fellow fetishists have their dreams fulfilled. Some are having their feet bitten; others are having razors drawn lightly through their skin. Many simply enjoy a foot massage or pedicure. Most, however, most . . .

There are cries and moans and yelps around him, but Georgie seems to be at peace, as he lies on the marble floor naked, stripped of inhibitions. Everyone is so wrapped up in themselves it is like he is not even there. He is a nonentity . . . . A nothing.

Georgie's face spasms, his eyes tighten. All his peace condenses into a single, surging spark. With one last, piteous moan, Georgie cums; his dick jerks. It is like a fountain, a continuous spurt. An everlasting orgasm. Perfection. It looks to him like he has splashed the red-haired, foot-smotherer—a small spot glistens brightly on her pinky toe.

And then it is over. She stands with one last suck, a parting flex of muscle, and then she is gone. Her white, broad bottom trotting swiftly away.

Georgie sighs and smiles.

Afterward, Georgie partakes in a foot trampling, an egg stomping, a salt crystal crawl. He wanders from room to room in the mansion, feeling the cool, sweet air conditioning on his naked skin. He is not worried about his penis, which shrivels to an embarrassing size in the chilled air. In this place, Georgie feels as invisible as anyone. Everyone is invisible, in this place.

(Parenthetical Pet Peeve) Glasses that fog up when you go outside from air-conditioned room, car, or building.

The foot trampling is fun as always, but still, Georgie would prefer to lie on the ground and have someone stomp him with her feet. Crush him under her strappy sandals. Georgie seems overwhelmed with pleasure, but doesn't feel quite satisfied. He longs for something else.

Rather than stomping on eggs, feeling the messy yolk and white exploding beneath his arch, he would rather be cracking the egg over someone else's foot, rubbing it in.

Georgie's own feet hold only momentary interest for him.

By late afternoon, Georgie needs more than what the mansion can offer. After much searching, he finally finds an ample-sized woman behind a small, out-of-the-way booth in the far corner of the first floor.

"I need something else," Georgie says. "This is all very nice, but . . . Well, it's just too nice," he explains.

He gives a smile to the woman behind the booth. He reminds himself that, even though she can clearly see him, he is still invisible.

The woman smiles back at him politely. She knows more about what happens in this place than anyone, yet she seems to see nothing at all of what is in front of her.

That is the secret to being a good front-desk clerk.

"Did you try the foot smothering?" she says. "Many of our clients find the foot smothering to be entirely satisfactory."

"Well, I tried it," Georgie admits, "but it's over now. I need more, now."

She nods in agreement. "Of course. Quite understandable." She glances over the multi-tiered schedule in front of her. "You are Georgie Gust?"

He nods.

The woman scrutinizes his day's schedule.

"I would much rather be walked on by other people's feet," Georgie says helpfully.

"Oh, I'm afraid we don't have much of that here," the woman sighs. She looks at Georgie appraisingly. "But I think I've found something that will work well for you. Yes. It's just the thing, really."

She points at a small square on the schedule, and Georgie leans over to take a look. His eyebrows rise.

"Starts in 15 minutes—either on the tennis courts or in the shed. Depending on whether you'd rather do it in the dark . . ." she drifts off.

Georgie nods enthusiastically.

"Thank you," he says.

"I'm here to serve." The woman smiles vacantly, her eyes seem to look miles and miles past him, as though Georgie is not really there at all.

Twelve minutes later, Georgie is standing in the doorway of the shed. It's dark inside, but he can hear the sounds of other masochists as they shift around within waiting for something to start.

Minutes pass. Georgie takes his place against the shed wall, watching the lighted doorway as a few other stragglers come in.

Then, there is a long shushing noise as a hard and granular substance pours out of a large container and onto the floor. Salt rock crystals, Georgie remembers. The bits of mineral ping slightly as they strike the hard cement floor.

The door slides closed and Georgie is plunged into utter darkness. The other masochists, who have been whispering and muttering amongst themselves the whole time, suddenly hold their collective breath. For a moment, there is silence.

A voice booms from the darkness: "Get down on your knees, filth!"

Georgie complies with joy. The salt rocks thrust up at him mightily from the floor.

"Now, crawl, like the vermin you are!" the voice booms.

Georgie and the others begin to move around. With every motion, the crystals bite into his skin and the salt begins to burn just beneath the surface. He moans at the pain, the degradation of it all. He hears his fellow crawlers moaning likewise, their voices released by his.

Before he knows it, the room is filled with groans and moans, the pitiable cries of help from the damned; the self-hating salt-crawlers. A part of Georgie longs to get sucked into the orgiastic swirl of pain, the communal hell that they have created. But another part of Georgie (Who? Me, Ben?) floats above him, and watches the scene despite the total darkness. Georgie foreshadows how pathetic he would become if he gave into the moment, if he got carried away with the passion of the crowd. And, seeing himself so clearly, he could not possibly allow himself to become anything else . . . especially a pathetic salt-crawler.

He is both interested and uninterested, enthralled and bored. The self-doubt, the worrying, begins to make him tire of the whole experience. It all falls short of the constant, never-ending orgasm he longs for. His appetite will accept nothing less.

Afterwards, back in his limo, Georgie is dressed anew, in white shirts and shorts, a black belt. He is filthy, yet clean. He sighs, unfulfilled.

His driver Ben glances at Georgie's knees, which are badly bruised.

"What happened to your legs?" Ben asks.

"Oh, that. I crawled on a floor covered with hard salt crystals."

Ben pauses a minute, seeming to assess Georgie's mood. He's been Georgie's chauffeur for five years; he knows his boss pretty well by now. He speaks again. Quietly. "And why did you do that?"

Georgie stares at his driver, whose face is reflected in the rearview mirror. He doesn't seem to judge.

"I don't know. It feels kind of good to crawl around on the ground. To feel pain."

Georgie is lying. It feels fucking great.

"Hmmm," Ben nods.

"It does!" Georgie insists. He realizes he might sound a little crazy.

"My nanny used to do all kinds of sick and twisted things to me," Georgie says quickly and defensively. "You know, like if I didn't do my homework or forgot to flush or something. Stupid shite like that."

"Oh, man, I'm sorry," Ben says. A canned response.

"Anyway, I'm all messed up about it," Georgie finishes lamely. "You know?"

"Yeah, that makes sense. Anyone would be," Ben says, nodding again.

There is a long, uncomfortable pause.

"I bet she was just jealous of you, all your money" Ben says finally. "It wasn't your fault, man."

"Yeah. Yeah! No shite."

Ben pulls the limousine slowly over to the side of the road. Georgie sags back in his seat, and then reaches to the floor between his legs and pulls out a self-help book, which he tosses to the other side of the car.

(Parenthetical Pet Peeve) Car alarms.

The limo stops; Georgie and Ben get out and lean against the back bumper, staring out at the desert. A tumbleweed blows by as Georgie takes a drag on his cigarette.

Ben exhales. "You know, somebody actually takes the time to think up all these fucked up ways of torturing other—keeping them in brightly lit rooms for days, like in Iraq, so that they lose their sense of time. Somebody actually sits down and imagines these twisted ways to warp people."

"Nanny used to get off to the torture stuff, she must have!" Georgie blurts.

That's sick. That's perfect, Georgie decides. But how could I get into that kind of shite? I should hate it more than anyone.

I'll fake it until I make it, until it works.

(It works if you work it.)

Ben sniffs. "Yeah, probably," he says. "You can't turn around these days without bumping into one sicko or another."

He blinks as his words register in his own mind, and glances swiftly at Georgie.

"She must have," Georgie mumbles.

It is clear Ben hasn't heard a word.

He tries to redeem himself. "But that's in the past," he says, playing counselor. "Maybe it's time to move on. To make something of your life, instead of letting your past own you."

Georgie scoffs. "Yeah, I'll make a mess is what I'll do."

"What is it that you want, Georgie, for real?" Ben insists. "You have everything a person needs and more."

And Georgie responds. "The never-ending orgasm. A peak experience that will last my lifetime. That's what I really want."

Georgie's face appears dreamy. He is in some other world, a roller coaster fantasy he can't escape.

Ben snorts and takes another drag. "Speaking of which, that woman you fancy—Margaret? Is she still employed as a helpline operator?"

Georgie waves his hand in front of his face, brushing Margaret off.

"Nah, she's old news," he says.

"Huh," says Ben. "She's the one you went to Tibet with, right?"

Georgie nods.

Ben raises an eyebrow. "Did you guys, uh . . ." He sneaks a quick look at Georgie. "Yeah?"

Georgie snorts. "'Course."

He is lying. They didn't.

"But that bitch, she's just so full of herself," he continues. "Walking around with that fucking holier-than-thou attitude . . . I swear, she's stalking me."

"It was pretty cool of her to go with you on the trip," Ben says.

Georgie gets what Ben means. "Yeah, I mean, she's great and all. Whatever. It's just she likes her job too much. She's one of *those* people."

"At least she has a job," Ben mutters.

(Parenthetical Pet Peeve) The fact that people have to play such dishonest games to get a job.

Georgie continues as if he hasn't heard. "I mean, who likes their job? She's so fucking happy all the time. Happy and fulfilled. That's Margaret. It makes me sick."

(Does it make you sick, Ben? Is that what makes you sick?

Shut up, Dr C. This is my story, see?)

"Yeah, I see what you mean," Ben says.

For a long time, they stay—leaning against the limo and staring out at the desert.

"So you're seeing someone else now?" Ben sniffs and spits softly from the side of his lips.

"Y-yeah. Kind of," Georgie says. He kicks at a tumbleweed that has embedded itself in the back tire of the limo. "My neighbor. Claudia."

Ben whistles and nods. "Nice," he says.

"Yeah?" Georgie sneaks a look at him. "Yeah, she's all right. She's so clingy, though, you know? I'm thinking about calling it quits."

"Hmm," Ben mutters, holding back a cough. "Sounds like you've got it all figured out," he says.

A few hours later, the limo pulls up in front of Georgie's bungalow.

Ben opens Georgie's door.

"See you later," he says.

Georgie gives a half-hearted wave as he unlocks the front door and walks in. The door closes behind him, and he is alone again.

Georgie glances at his answering machine; it sits silent and dark. He presses the play button anyway.

"You have no new messages," the machine chimes.

Georgie turns the shower on and proceeds to shuffle around his filthy living room in the near twilight.

The room is an overkill of every fancy modernization, every electronic doodad, and every entertainment gadget he could possibly squeeze in. There are photos and drawings framed across the walls of every past girlfriend. The bookshelves boast awards, trophies, and posters from his travels. There are seriously intellectual books— endless piles of them—most of them in three copies. His video and music collections feature an equivalent overabundance.

He owns an absurd assortment of things. Sketches and notes are left lying around, some only half-complete. His drawings and paintings are scattered, unfinished, but still indicative of brilliance.

Then, there are the graph paper illustrations; intricate designs clearly drawn with some vague purpose. It's obvious that Georgie has a strong mind, maybe too strong for his own good. He also has an exorbitant number of projects in process—arbitrary projects, redundant and grandiose.

The elements of his house, although artistic, are placed according to obscure mathematical relationships. Everything somehow corresponds. Quantum physics material is neatly clustered, labeled, and placed with the complementary videos and books; an MC Escher print hangs in close proximity.

(Parenthetical Pet Peeve) The valuing of form over function, image over substance in modern society, the fact that Albert Einstein would likely have a hard time getting a job himself if he were alive today due to his messy hair and wore ratty clothing.

Similarly, his stationary bike is surrounded by trophies, workout tapes, sports magazines, and signed baseballs.

The metal ceiling fan reflects light while it spins slowly above the bike. Georgie peeks out the window, hoping to catch a glimpse of Claudia. He rushes over and crouches by the curtains when he hears the door to her house open and close. He wonders if she notices him watching, and wonders whether she counts on the fact that he stares, still waiting. Waiting for her. Waiting for something.

Maybe she is showering. Maybe she has forgotten her towel and will have to walk through the living room naked.

He thinks of sucking on her hooker-blue toenails. They taste like candy.

She is not home. Her house sits empty and dark.

Georgie returns to the running shower, which is now steaming.

He daydreams in the shower, even when the soap falls. He doesn't wash his hair today, remembering someone somewhere once told him: *You never look your best when you meet the one you've been waiting for your entire life. You are never completely prepared for that.*

Georgie resolves to never be fully prepared.

"No sex. Love," Georgie mutters in the shower. "She must've thought of me as the friendly type. That's fine. I'm used to it."

He picks up the bar of soap, runs it over his hair, and rinses out the suds.

"I enjoyed myself, that's all that matters."

Georgie can see God laughing at him, taking delight in Claudia's orchestration of him, that day. That one day, that one eternal day she and he met. The day they were together.

A pensive pause. An epiphany.

"I'll call it personal growth," he tells the walls of the shower. "I'll never hear from Claudia, ever again."

He runs the bar of soap over his hair and rinses out the suds, forgetting he already has.

"My mind ran wild with quiet confusion. It soothed the senses. I could wake up tomorrow, thinking about that day, and the next day about today," he mutters. "While I'm in love, I stop writing, for the most part. I know it won't last forever. I'm in love: I scoff at the thought. Me? In love? In love with Claudia? Me? In love with Claudia . . . ."

Georgie's alarm clock is set for 10:00 am. It blares and blares. He dreams of fires, and sirens. He tosses and turns.

Eventually, the bright white light of the afternoon light shines through his blinds.

Georgie crawls out of bed. The clock mocks him. It's 2:00 pm.

Georgie shuffles into the kitchen. He's a wreck. He pulls a mug from the sink and inspects the inside.

Not too bad, he thinks, again. Just a little grungy around the edges. Kind of like me.

Georgie mopes around and stares blankly. He can't sleep. There's no use sleeping, he thinks, when your every need is attended to. No use in resting when you never exert yourself.

For days on end he stares at the ceiling, at the wall-fan, at Claudia's driveway and her empty windows.

It all boils down to nothing, and he leaves for the grocery store.

"Georgie!" Margaret calls, waving.

(Doesn't this bitch ever go home?)

Briefly, Georgie thinks about leaving, racing out the doors and back home. Instead, he grumbles and plucks a jar of pickles from the shelf in front of him.

"Georgie," she says again, rolling her cart up to his. "How are you doing?"

"Great. Just great," he answers. "How's everything with you?"

"Oh, the same," she says. There is an awkward pause. Georgie scans the nutrition facts on the back of the pickle jar. Meanwhile, Margaret seems to be weighing whether it would be better to buy generic or go for the brand name.

"What do you think about the riots?" she finally says, at a loss.

"Huh?"

Georgie examines an entire wall of mustard.

"The riots. On the news? I'm glad that it's not on our side of town."

"I don't really watch the news." Georgie replies.

"Oh." Margaret looks stunned but only for a second.

"Well you should really look into it," she says brightly. "The east side is getting so crowded now—unemployment, you know—and they're starting to form crowds and . . . and you know they burned down the First Methodist Church, don't you?"

Georgie shakes his head.

"You don't! Georgie, you need to get up to speed. Like I said, who knows when this might start to affect our neighborhood."

"Someone actually takes the time to think up this shite," he mumbles, choosing the store brand Dijon.

"What? Well, yeah." Margaret gives Georgie a searching glance.

He tries to appear normal.

"Anyway, it's all about unemployment and the lack of services for the poor. Crime is through the roof now, on the east side, you know. There's this whole Robin Hood mentality . . . ."

"She must've gotten off to it," Georgie mumbles. "She just had to."

Margaret searches his face. "Who?"

(Claudia . . .)

"What?" Georgie looks at her face. "What are you talking about?"

Margaret blinks. Once. Twice.

"Hey, Georgie, let's get together sometime this week," she suggests, a sympathetic, almost pitying look on her face.

"Yeah, yeah. Sure." he agrees, thinking to himself it'll never happen. He'll pull his shades down, pretend he's not home.

"I'll drop by Wednesday," insists Margaret. She pats his hand lightly. "You sure you're doing okay?"

She smiles. Always with the smiling. Does she ever stop?

"Yeah, yeah. Great," he replies, convincingly.

With that, she saunters off.

Dear Diary:

I went to the doctor's office today. My doctor asked me, "Does anyone in your family suffer from insanity? I grinned and said, "No, we all enjoy it!"

Making it Count With Dr C

"Who is Margaret, really, Ben? Who is Claudia?" Dr C asks, crossing her slender legs. Her eyes are steady on me. She thinks she sees right through me, knows all my deepest, darkest secrets.

She doesn't know the worst of them.

"Whaddaya mean, Dr C," I tease her. "Margaret's Margaret. Claudia's Claudia."

She nods and leans forward. "I know that. In Georgie's world, that's who they are. But who are they really, Ben? In your world."

Dr C is going deep now. I can tell. Not that it will get her anywhere.

"They're nothing in my world, Dr C. In my world, they don't even exist. That's the beauty of it, you see?"

Dr C sighs. She often wears that dreamy expression when attempting to connect to me on a human level. She leans further forward and her breasts are almost touching my knees.

Yeah, she has my attention now. Maybe I'm the one that gets to go deep this time, huh?

But no. Her holy nipples never make contact. Nor her feet, which I notice are decked out in those red sling-backs. She wants me, wants to seduce me. Tempting me like that. With her tits. Her feet.

"What I mean, Ben," she says, "is do they represent people in your own life? Of all people, why does Georgie meet them? What does he need from them?"

"Why does anybody meet anybody, Dr C? It's all damn fool luck, as far as I'm concerned."

"What do you get out of it, Ben?" she says. It's her attempt to redirect me, put the conversation back on track, back where she wants it.

"What?" I say.

"Out of knowing Georgie. Out of being Georgie. What do you get out of it?"

I stare at her for a moment, blinking nine times. Now she is acting like the crazy one. I may like to take a hop every now and then, may have a bit of a stutter, but even I do not believe that I chose Georgie any more than I believe he chose me.

"I appreciate the company?" I suggest.

Dr C shakes her head slow and heavy. She sighs. "You are not being very helpful, Ben," she says.

There is a moment of silence between us.

"It's not like I chose him, you know," I say finally. There, Dr C. Have a gem.

"Huh?" she mutters, lifting her head slightly.

"Georgie. I didn't wake up one day and decide: 'Hey, you know what would be cool? Having an alter ego. I'll make one up. Call him Georgie.' It didn't happen that way, Dr C."

"Well, of course not, Ben. I would not dare suggest that you did this consciously."

"What happened is: One day I woke up, and there he was. Right next to me. In bed. His head on the same goddamn pillow. I was him. He was me. And that was the end of that. Bam! Now we're stuck with each other."

"You're right, Ben. I'm sorry."

At this, I reel back. The chair I'm in doesn't have wheels. It tips back and falls over, with me along for the ride.

The pain doesn't bother me so much. Not so much as hearing those words from her mouth.

"Uh, what?" I say from the floor, rubbing my head. One, two, three times.

Maybe I misheard. Maybe it's some sort of audio hallucination. Maybe it's just the concussion, talking.

"I am sorry, Ben," she repeats. "You're right. It's lousy of me to expect you'll give me all the answers. I'm just tired, I suppose."

"It's o-okay," I stutter. I lift myself back into the chair, keeping a constant eye on her.

"Why don't you just pick up where you left off?" she prompts me, smiling, "We'll figure it out sooner or later. Don't you worry."

I shrug. "Sure."

Dear Diary:

I think my latest bouts with chronic insomnia are more a mental disorder than a medical disease of the body to be solved with meds. Likely caused by my other conditions, yet appearing to be a control issue—with control being determined by the mind.

Claudia Goes Deep

Later that night, it begins to rain. Georgie rushes to the window as he hears a car door slam outside Claudia's house. He watches as she stomps to her front door with no regard for the wetness. She tears the door open and slams it shut behind her, then turns on every light in the house. He aches for a glimpse of her shadow to fall on the curtains.

(Parenthetical Pet Peeve) While getting packages out of the car, the car door swings back and swats you on the rump.

Her figure pauses, standing still for a moment. Then she's back out the door.

Georgie stares as she stomps back to her car. His groin tightens as she turns up the sidewalk and then . . . up his driveway. His driveway.

He looks around frantically, grabs a handful of wrappers from the coffee table, and shoves them in his pocket. He paces once, twice. The wreck of his life is too bright, too visible, to anyone who comes through the front door. He turns off the overhead light.

Claudia's fist pounds on the front door.

He opens the door wide.

"You wouldn't believe the piece of shite day I've had." She barges through the open door, shucking off her wet jacket and handing it to him.

"Yeah?" Georgie asks. He drops her jacket onto a chair by the door.

Claudia sways and barely catches herself with a hand on his sofa.

"Can I sit?" She doesn't seem to notice the squalor.

"Yeah, yeah." Georgie moves a pile of papers and books from one end of the sofa to the other. Claudia collapses into the cushions. Her eyes briefly close.

"Um, are you thirsty?" Georgie asks.

"You got any vodka?" Her voice already slurred.

"Kahlua," he answers.

"Perfect."

Quickly, Georgie pulls a dirty glass from the sink, wipes it with a wet paper towel, and fills it with ice cubes and Kahlua.

"Here" He hands it to her. She smiles and takes a long, slow sip.

"A little dark in here, isn't it?" she says slowly.

Georgie looks around. If he turns on the main light, she'll see the true depth of his slovenliness. Instead, he lights a few candle stubs on the coffee table.

"I lost my job today," she ultimately confesses. "Those fucking bastards fired me."

(Parenthetical Pet Peeve) Resume bullshit. I write, "I coordinated all company communications," when all I did was answer the phones.

Georgie racks his brains, trying to remember how normal people respond to a crisis. *(Normal? Who's normal?)*

"I'm sorry," he says, after a long pause, trying to sympathize.
(That's what normal people do, right? They sympathize.)
"What happened?" he asks.

"Those motherfuckers." She gulps the Kahlua and looks around the room. She's distracted, Georgie decides. That's all. Just distracted.

"I shouldn't have fucked him," she says. "Greg. In case you're wondering. That's who I shouldn't have fucked. It's just like my dad always said, 'Don't shite where you eat.' But who listens to their father? Jesus."

"Oh," Georgie says, as bile rises in his throat at the thought of her with another man. His penis jerks a little, a cock tic. "Who's Greg?"

"Greg was my co-worker; my boss, actually. At the clinic. Fucking pig. He was married, you know, but I didn't care. I mean it was sex. Just sex. Fucking. I couldn't have cared less 'about him or his bitch of a wife—'""

Georgie interrupts. "Which clinic?"

Claudia looks at him quizzically. "Mt Shasta," she says. "I'm a paramedic."

"Oh, good," Georgie says, and then snaps his mouth shut.
(At least it's not . . .
Not what, Ben?
You'll see, you'll see . . .)

She shrugs. "Yeah, it wasn't too bad. But when I broke it off with him and Sara—"

Again Georgie interrupts. "Who's Sara?"

"His wife," Claudia says. "I was doing them both, actually. It was fun."

Georgie's mind reels. A married man and his wife? This woman is a mess. She sits there on his couch in all her mascara-streaked glory, her wild hair curling in a scarlet halo—sits there, in her perverted glory, her sexual freedom, her misery. Her overripe breasts sag just like the couch.

She's perfect, Georgie thinks.

(Parenthetical Pet Peeve) Jobs that are a professional appearance, but don't pay a professional salary to go with it—especially for young girls.

"Anyway, when it all blew up, when it all got . . . personal . . . they fired me. He fucking fired me!" She picks up a drawing from the pile of papers next to her and blows her nose into it. She crinkles up the precious thing—the fragile child of Georgie's genius, now covered in her snot—and throws it across the room.

(Perfect . . .)

"Sounds like a creep," Georgie says, in what he hopes is a sage tone. "It's probably a good thing you don't work for him anymore."

Claudia laughs, a tad hysterically. "Sure. That makes sense."

She lifts the Kahlua to her mouth and drinks deep. She sighs and relaxes into the sofa.

"I just want to hurt him," she says softly. "Punch him in the face, slice up his arm, his junk. Make him crawl naked on glass, cut him. Make him bleed. Then he'd know how I feel!" She kicks the coffee table, hard. The corner of it lifts high and the candles and a stack of papers go flying. One of the candles lands on a stack of paper and hisses out. The other lands on Georgie's lap.

"Ow!" he howls, standing and shaking the hot wax from his groin in the suddenly dark room. His heart pounds with the jolt of fear and adrenaline rushes through his veins. His cock jerks slightly.

"Oh shite, oh shite, I'm so sorry," Claudia says. She slides to her knees in front of him, wiping at the crotch of his pants with her hands, clumsily fumbling.

They're lit only by the scanty moonlight that shines through the clouds. Georgie thinks he can see her blush.

"Shite. Are you okay?"

Georgie nods, then smiles. *(Bliss.)* That rush was just what he needed, somehow.

Claudia can't know that, of course. And in the darkness she can't see him smiling.

"That hurt!" he says, crossing his arms in front of his chest and frowning down at her, wanting to see her squirm.

She looks abashed, sorrowful. "I'm sorry!"

Georgie's dick stands at attention to hear her sorrow.

She is perfect in her misery.

Why do I like her best this way? he wonders. What kind of sicko prefers to see a woman cry?

(That's a good question, Ben.

It's not me, Dr C. It's Georgie, see?)

Georgie is struck suddenly by (what he thinks is) the greatest idea of his life. He sits down next to Claudia, his thigh hot up against hers. Then he leans over and kisses her softly on the mouth.

She returns the kiss with feeling.

Georgie breaks it off. They stare at each other a minute.

"That felt kind of good," Claudia admits quietly. "When I burned you. You're not Greg, but . . . it felt kind of good, anyway. Is that sick or what?"

Georgie laughs to himself.

"I've got an idea," he says. "It might sound crazy at first but just hear me out. You're out of a job, now. You've got bills to pay. And me? Well, I need someone . . . someone like you."

He smiles again, his face almost invisible in the darkness.

When Claudia wakes up the next morning, the sun shines brightly through Georgie's slatted blinds. She reaches out her hand to the empty space beside her then sits up. Georgie is gone.

She blinks her eyes once, twice. Then she looks at the nightstand as her eyes widen slightly.

The clock reads: 9:00 am.

There is a high stack of hundred dollar bills beside it.

(Where's Georgie, Ben?

I don't know, Dr C. Can't a guy have a little privacy?)

And next to the money, a note on lined paper. Folded. Once. Twice. Three times. Claudia pulls at it, pulls at the note.

It is so bright in the light of day that she can hardly read it. She leans back into the pillow and holds the note above her head, making a shadow on the page.

Dear Claudia, (the note reads)

As per our agreement last night, here is your weekly allowance.

Claudia thumbs through the stack of hundreds, counting out a full 10. She smiles. Then she returns her attention to the note.

There are, of course, a few vital stipulations:

1. Thou shall not have sexual relationships with anyone but me.

2. Real money must be exchanged for any and all favors.

3. Failure to comply with the above shall result in double pay or loss of job.

(Parenthetical Pet Peeve) Pay cuts.

This discreet contract will never expire, until death.

Yours,

Georgie Gust

Claudia frowns as she looks at the note, then glances over at the wad of cash that has slumped slightly against her leg. She grabs the cash, thumbing through it once again. Then she crumples up the note and throws it in the trash.

Dear Diary:

Marking third day of insomnia, this condition has a mind of its own as a third party, influencing my own authenticity and reality & perhaps of our own individual colorful natures, as I see in my friends. In "confession" of mania, flitting feelings of spontaneous confessional prose spewing like Jack Kerouac writing *On the Road*, or as Carrie Fisher described her feeling as if a "light bulb in a world of moths," regardless of today's work and stresses, I continue my commitment to doing what I feel, and keeping it real, and in the now. My commitment to self: to stay in the heart of my heart, where all the healing and wholeness resides, and to remain just as I am; myself. This rare mental health condition I'm presented with often fascinates me incredibly; the mental challenges often faced & overcome. To seize the day again, in lieu of feeling guilt, apology or uncertainty for yesterday—the past, nor to anticipate tomorrow, in confession of such inspiration having derived from a product of stress & over-work . . . I move forward. I move ahead.

Ah, What a Comfy Web They Weave . . .

Georgie and Claudia get right to business. Claudia comes over later that week, with a pair of handcuffs, a feather duster, a roll of duct tape, and a waxing kit. She clinks the handcuffs together mischievously.

"Hey there, Georgie Gust," she pouts and tips forward slightly, emphasizing her breasts. "Want to come play?"

Georgie nods his head mutely. It all looks pretty kitsch to him, but then Claudia is new at the whole torture thing. In a way, she is now a virgin.

Georgie smiles up at her as she straddles him on the bed.

"What are you thinking, Mr Gust?" she says in mock shock. She closes the handcuff around one of his hands and loops the empty cuff through the holes in his headboard.

"That you're a virgin," Georgie says, wanting to share with her, to make an open forum. Like when he gave her his first pedicure. He wants it to be like that.

"Oh, hardly," Claudia grins and locks the other handcuff into place. She slides off the bed and shimmies out of her too-tight jeans.

"Not s-sexually, I mean," Georgie stutters. "Uh, an S&M virgin. A virgin torturer."

"Oh, Georgie." Claudia sinks to the side of the bed, checking the temperature of the hot wax with her hand. She smiles to find that it is right.

"This may be my first time with a pair of handcuffs . . . ." She places a hand over Georgie's mouth as he smiles.

"But that doesn't mean it's my first time torturing someone."

She slowly stuffs the feather duster into his mouth. The feathers soak up the moisture of his tongue and stick to the roof of his mouth. They flutter against the back of his throat, making him cough.

Georgie tries to protest the feathers, but all that comes out is an indistinct mumble and a frustrated moan. Clamping the feather duster down with her forearm, Claudia uses the duct tape to fix it onto his face.

"There, that should keep your gag reflex from getting in the way," she purrs. "Isn't that nice?"

Georgie rapidly shakes his head. His panic sets off another coughing fit; he chokes, coughs, and sneezes until he can't open his eyes anymore because of the tears streaming from them, until his face is red with frustration.

"If you don't calm down, you won't enjoy the rest of this," Claudia points out, pouting. She has a dipstick covered in the hot wax, letting it drip down onto Georgie's stomach.

"Just hold your breath for a while," she suggests.

He does as she asks, and eventually the feathers that tormented his tonsils are still. Georgie is now able to enjoy the feel of the warm wax as it drips onto him.

It's not too hot at all, more like a warm bath. He swims in the wax, feeling it engulf him.

He thinks of it coating his whole body, spreading up from his toes and over his genitals, up to his belly button, armpits, then up over his face, running into his mouth and locking his tongue in place, and gluing his eyeballs to a fixed stare.

Then he would be dead, but forever existing.

They could prop him up in a wax museum.

He would be famous, and he would not even have to deal with the consequences. The people. Wanting him. Wanting to be with him, touch him, get his autograph.

Georgie indulges these fantasies as Claudia spreads the wax over him. She sings a little tune under her breath as she works. After a while, Georgie is able to entirely forget that the feather duster is in his mouth. He thinks about a little girl pointing to his waxen testicles and asking: "Mommy, what are those?"

"Those are peanuts, dear," the mommy replies.

Fantasies only last so long, however, and Claudia is still spreading and spreading when Georgie runs out of imaginary material.

Georgie starts to wonder if Claudia doesn't have what it takes to be his torturer. This wax stuff is not half bad. But it's not bad enough.

Maybe Samantha, down on that place at Third Street, would be better. She gives one hell of a good foot smothering.

Then, Georgie receives a slight twinge of understanding. Claudia tugs at a bit of hardened wax down by his ankle. And it hurts. A little. The anticipation of greater pain gets him breathing faster. He almost inhales the feathers, almost chokes again.

"Better stay calm, Georgie dear," Claudia reminds him.

She crouches over his body, holding herself just inches above him. Her nose is almost touching his, her breath is on his face.

"All women are torturers," she snarls. "It's in our nature."

Without looking, she catches her nail where the wax stops at his collarbone and gives a swift yank.

"Gmma!" Georgie yells through a mouthful of feathers. Then he starts to cough again.

"We know exactly what it is you are afraid of," she continues, ignoring him. "We know exactly how to hurt you."

She tears off another small piece.

There are no strips! Georgie realizes. He doesn't know much about waxing, not any more than the average male human, but he does know that strips are involved. And with no strips . . . she is going to have to pull off every inch of it by hand. Every round little inch.

Georgie stifles a groan, not wanting the feathers to act up again.

"Men may be stronger, Georgie," Claudia concludes. "But women are the true inflictors of pain."

She rips up a quarter-sized chunk of wax affixed to his nipple, and Georgie howls. The feathers dive down his throat. He chokes, coughing and yelling and cursing Claudia in the best way he can.

Oh, what a woman! Some part of his mind praises her.

Something seems to snap in Claudia. Her eyes are suddenly full of rage. "How does that feel, huh? Does it hurt?" She tears off piece after piece, faster and faster now, until it feels like Georgie's entire torso is enflamed. She stops for a moment, gets back in his face.

"This is what women do to make themselves beautiful for you!" she screams at him, her face red and terrible. She tears off another piece, a dollar-coin sized piece right near his groin. "Am I beautiful enough for you, Georgie?"

She tears and tears at him, at the wax, not paying attention, not even caring where the wax ends and Georgie begins. His pores scream in pain. His skin is covered in thousands of tiny scratches and a few sizeable gouges from her ripping. He bleeds. It is horrible; he's terrified. At the same time, a sense of peace flows over him. He feels detached from his own body, and watches safely from a distance.

He feels sorry for Claudia, who is clearly unhappy.

Feels a little ashamed for taking advantage of her unhappiness.

But only a little.

Mostly, he feels a blissful sort of numbness.

He wishes he could ejaculate, but his cock is encased in hard wax.

Finally, Claudia collapses over him, sobbing. Incoherent. Georgie steadies his breathing, wondering what comes next.

It's almost half an hour before Claudia's breathing slows, before her shuddering ceases. Then she looks up at him, with wide, illuminated irises. Her eyes are wet and glowing. She is beautiful.

"I'm tired of this," she says. With a sniff, she stands and leaves the room.

She leaves Georgie tied to the bedpost, his legs and genitals hopelessly covered in wax, the feather duster taped securely in his mouth.

Huh, Georgie thinks as he watches her go. I wasn't expecting that.

Only minutes later, Georgie realizes that his peanuts itch.

"Biiiiiiiitch!!!" he screams up from somewhere in his belly. He enunciates with his esophagus, so the whole neighborhood can hear and understand. Then he chokes and coughs, snorting and hiccupping and sobbing until exhaustion overcomes him and he passes out.

(Parenthetical Pet Peeve) Hiccupping.

Claudia hears his final screams, his despair, his infinite pain.

The shitey thing about empathy, Claudia realizes, is that even when you're torturing someone, you can feel it yourself.

Otherwise you wouldn't know how good it works.

Claudia is not sure if she can handle this job. She loves the feel of Georgie's pain, loves the preparation of it, loves his screams and the sense of vindication that it brings her.

But then there is the pain, too. Claudia's not quite sure she can handle the pain.

When Georgie wakes up, he is free of the wax, feather duster, and handcuffs.

He has no idea how that could have happened. Well, he has three ideas:

Claudia might have pulled off the rest of the wax and his subconscious mind blocked it out.

Or:

Claudia might have drugged him so he wouldn't feel pain and peeled away the wax.

Or:

Claudia might have melted the wax, somehow, and poured it into a bucket.

(Well which is it, Ben? Inquiring minds . . .

How am I supposed to know, Dr C? You think I'm psychic or something?)

After that night, Claudia disappears. For days, Georgie stalks her house, peeking through the blinds. But she is nowhere to be seen. He calls and leaves message after message—all left unreturned. A week passes.

Georgie leaves her allowance in the mailbox.

He's afraid that maybe she took the first thousand and ran. Maybe she doesn't want to play his game. This fear of rejection—the terror of another failed relationship, no matter how forced—fills him with a mixture of hatred for her, the power she has to make him ill, and a longing that feels a little bit like love.

(Have you ever been in love, Dr C?)

Fear and uncertainty give him a pain that sets him free, that fills him with delicious, slimy horror. He can't get enough of the pain her disappearance brings him. If she abandoned him forever, he might slide deeper and deeper into the cold and empty abyss, the nothingness of self that echoes. Oh, perfectly, that everlasting moment of orgasm.

Although he is spying every moment, waiting for her, he doesn't see the moment she comes, doesn't see her remove the money. And yet it is gone the next day.

Georgie smiles to himself. A feeling even better than pain flushes through his veins.

It is triumph.

Soon after the money mysteriously disappears from the mailbox, Claudia begins to show up at her house now and then. Still, she doesn't return his calls, or come to visit, or write any notes to him. But he knows that she is there, sometimes, and she knows that he knows.

This is a new kind of torture, a new delicious pain. He knows she is still playing. The question now is not "if" but "when." And as the days drag on, Georgie becomes increasingly impatient. He makes a permanent camp in the living room, keeping everything necessary for survival next to the window, within reach of his hands. He lives for glimpses of Claudia through the blinds. Sometimes, in the dark, he imagines her naked, thinks of the softness of her sagging breasts falling to either side of her chest as she sleeps.

As the days go by with no Claudia showing up, Georgie begins to run out of food. He makes runs to the kitchen to refill his water, but when the cupboards are bare he forgets the water too, and sits and sits, watching. Slowly, he begins to starve, dehydrate, melt away into the air. He feels his skin slowly tightening around him, feels the water leaving his body to feed the atmosphere. He sighs, waiting and waiting for Claudia to show up.

Eventually, Georgie becomes too weak to leave money for her in the mailbox. He slumps against the windowpane, his gaze propped up only by his nose at the sill.

The next day, there's a knock at his door.

(Parenthetical Pet Peeve) Door-to-door salespeople.

Georgie swivels his gaze to the door, knowing somehow, just knowing that it is Claudia. But there's no need to answer it, he thinks to himself. She'll come to me.

Then the door is silent, and Georgie feels a sustained moment of terror. That was my chance, that was my only chance, and I blew it.

She's gone now, gone forever.

And I can't lift a finger.

The terror is replaced with a sense of bliss, the orgasmic nothingness of despair. Georgie melts into it, happy to disappear. God takes pleasure in this. Claudia will not miss Georgie, not his orchestration or his loving, playful orders. She'll enjoy her freedom. It is best.

The knock comes again at his door, louder and more insistent. Georgie realizes that it has awakened him from sleep. He has fallen to a heap on the floor, lacking the energy to even prop his nostrils at the windowsill.

He thinks for a moment about answering the door. He decides that he likes the numbness better. His ear sags down to the floor.

The door is pounding, shaking under the power of Claudia's fist.

"Georgie, I know you're in there!" she yells. "I know you're in there!"

Georgie flashes back to Ben's mother, to her voice feather-light in the dark doorway of Ben's childhood bedroom.

"I know you're in there," Ben's mother whispers. Georgie shivers.

"I know you're in there, Benjy . . . ."

A crash of glass and Georgie screams, his voice high like a little girl's. He feels the last bit of life in him leave with that scream. It sounds like a whisper amid the tinkling of glass all around him.

"Damnit, Georgie, what did you think you were doing?" Claudia mutters. She hoists him in her arms.

He is thin, starved, emaciated, jaundiced, and sleep-deprived. Unshowered, swollen boils and pustules adorn his thighs; he has been too exhausted to pop them. His semen-crusted pubes show a history of careless masturbation.

(Parenthetical Pet Peeve) Dieting.

"Poor little Georgie!" murmurs Claudia. "My little paranoid poopsy. I can smell you rotting away!"

He is like a child in her arms, although she never had one. A child, that is . . . .

Georgie awakens in the white sterility of a hospital bedroom. He screams, closing his eyes. His shout is loud, clear, and resounding.

"Georgie!" Claudia cries. She has been sitting next to his bed.

Well, isn't that sweet? some part of his brain snarls.

"What the fuck?" Georgie sits up straight in bed and then collapses backward. A nurse pokes her head into the room.

"Get me the fuck out of here!" Georgie yells, his eyes bulging. The nurse's head withdraws, and she scurries away.

"Georgie, calm down," Claudia tries to shush him. "You're in the hospital. You almost died. You'll be all right. Maybe in a day or two."

Georgie looks at the tangle of cords, ignoring Claudia.

"Why didn't you eat, or buy any food or anything, Georgie?" she asks.

Georgie can see from her face that she knows the answer. She wants it not to be her fault.

Fuck that shite.

Without her guilt, her repentance, this whole arrangement would be nothing better than the fetish houses he used to attend.

And at least at the houses there is a bit of variety.

He finds the clamp on his finger that measures his pulse and rips it off. He smiles sweetly as the blip-blip of the heart monitor begins to sing like a siren.

Nurses, doctors, oxygen therapists rush into the room. They glare at Georgie's sweet smile.

"Get me the fuck out of here," he tells them. "I will pay to have all of this moved to my house. See her?" He gestures to Claudia with an evil glare. "She's my live-in caretaker."

Claudia's eyes bulge, but she dares not refute him.

"I'm a paramedic," she explains. "Mt Shasta—"

The nurses sniff their disapproval, but the doctor eventually approves the arrangement. Claudia can't help but notice how much thicker the doctor's front pocket seems after his interview with Georgie.

Despite all his problems, Georgie can be very persuasive.

Hours later, Georgie is nestled snugly in his home, surrounded by wires and monitors. His heart rate beeps pleasantly. Claudia is dressed in a sexy nurse's uniform, tending to his every whim. For the occasion, she has moved into the room next to his. Just until his health returns, of course.

Once the hospital realized who he was, whose son he was, it seemed they could not get rid of Georgie fast enough. It helped that Georgie pulled a wad of hundreds out of his wallet—a wallet thicker than Claudia's wrist.

"You look good in that," Georgie leers, as Claudia leans over to place a tray of food on his lap. The heart rate monitor speeds up slightly.

"Why, thank you," Claudia simpers. She doesn't really mind the situation, and she likes the way the outfit shows off her figure.

Lunch served, Claudia sits in the chair beside Georgie's bed and crosses her legs, showing her bare thighs, visible through the slits on each side of her skirt. Freckles dotting her legs smile at him through the slits, teasing/inviting him. Her skin wrinkles slightly—just enough.

"Mind if I smoke?" she asks, already pulling the pack out of her purse.

"Does it matter?" Georgie reminds her.

She assesses him carefully, shrugs, and then lights a slim cigarette. She exhales into his face.

Georgie coughs, feeling a faint rush of happiness at his discomfort.

Claudia smiles a Mona Lisa smile, even though she feels momentary doubt when she sees Georgie cough. Part of her doesn't like to see his discomfort, but a larger part wants to hurt him and all men forever and ever (amen)—to twist him and grind him into a pitiful nothingness.

His evident pleasure reassures her that what she has done is good.

It's good for me, good for both of us, she reminds herself.

"You know what I like about taking care of you here?" she asks, smiling wickedly.

"What?" Georgie asks.

Her eyebrows raise, innocent. "The fact that we're alone," she says. Then slowly she drops her hand and grinds her cigarette butt into his arm. Georgie screams. She closes her eyes to pull his pain closer to her. She gives one last twist, feeling the ember crush into empty ash.

Claudia leans back in her chair as Georgie slumps into his pillows. She takes a few deep breaths then feels for his pulse.

His heart is still strong, despite all that he has been through.

Claudia lays herself down at Georgie's side, closing her eyes. Just for a minute . . . .

It is exhausting, taking care of Georgie. She is not just his nurse, after all. She is also his torturer—his personal trainer in pain. She has to ensure she gives him that high he craves and satisfy her own perverse longings; all the while she must be certain it's not too much for him right now. His heart must remain stable, and his body can't go into shock.

The situation requires her to summon all her knowledge as a paramedic and then to go entirely against her training.

She wonders if Georgie took into consideration her medical training when he decided to choose her for his torturer. It would be handy to have a professional on hand, someone who understood the limits of the human body.

She doubts it. It is much more likely that her body, her face, her unique situation made her far more qualified in Georgie's mind than any medical experience would.

"You're one lucky son of a bitch, picking me," Claudia whispers to him gently. "Any other bimbo would have killed you already, or have just taken the money and run."

Claudia breathes deeply and evenly, comforted by the sound of Georgie's heartbeat.

In a little while she will get back to work. But not just yet . . . .

"Georgie," Claudia whispers. He opens his eyes to see her crouched above him like a predatory animal. The buttons of her uniform are open; her simple, pink nipples loom over his forehead.

"Ah, there you are," she says quietly. She reaches down between his legs and strokes the bulge in his pants. She smiles. "Right there?"

He lifts his arm weakly; the wires drag him back down.

"It's all right, it's all right," she shushes him. With a small smile, she puts her hands on his arms, pinning him down beneath her. She kisses him full on the mouth, nibbling at his lips and drawing a little blood. Georgie moans in ecstasy.

With fingers like fire ants, Claudia unzips Georgie's pants. She fumbles his stiffening man dagger away from the hot swamp of his crotch. She pinches the soft skin of his balls with her fingernails.

Georgie cries out in pain and joy. He lifts his head and then, with a sigh, leans back into the pillow.

"That's good," he says.

"I thought you'd like that," Claudia murmurs. She pinches him again, harder. Tears ball up in the corners of his eyes.

When his lids flutter open again, Claudia slowly strips out of her nurse's uniform. Her breasts sag easily against her chest, enticing him. Her skin is pink, spotted with freckles and pores, covered in long, thin, shimmery red hairs. Her carpet matches the drapes, a wild, orange-red, waving him in. His dick is full of blood, thick with it. He thinks it might burst open at any minute.

Georgie sees her red, dangling lips that glisten, wet for him. He strains for her.

"Condoms. In the drawer," he gasps.

Claudia laughs low, almost purring. "Hm?" she says, pressing herself up against him.

"No!" Georgie moans. "The condoms. Please. God, please."

Claudia slowly, inexorably, sinks his shaft inside herself.

"Please?" he whimpers.

"Oh, no," she shushes him. "You don't get it that easy."

Georgie realizes this is part of the game. She is torturing him with contact, invading his sterile existence. What if she gets pregnant? Gets pregnant? Pregnant? Something screams inside him as she pushes against him, deeper and deeper. There is no protection between them, no safe place. If a child results from her torture, she doesn't care.

The fear of this possibility, of her not caring, of the risk—real risk—rises up in him and bursts.

"Yeeeaah?" he murmurs as he comes inside her, hard. She laughs at him. And for a moment, Georgie feels it—that sweet, endless bliss he has been searching for. He laughs along with her, pulling her face down with his plugged-in arms.

Maybe this is it, Georgie thinks. Maybe this is all I've been looking for.

I could get used to this.

Dear Diary:

I'm a narcissist. Many have pointed this out and I've assumed as such years ago, I am aware of my narcissism. "Charming, loveable, inspiring," also, might I add, and I (I-I-I-!!!) often joke about it (or feel guilty about it) but knowing that part of the definition of narcissism is one with no self-esteem (because technically one can't have low or high levels of self-esteem—one either has self-esteem, or not, as I see and know self-esteem). It's not intentional. It's perhaps the "Sheldon Cooper" in me, from *The Big Bang Theory* on TV. Zooey Deschanel's sister, Emily Deschanel, in the show Bones, as well. Many say I remind them of her character, Dr Temperance 'Bones' Brennan, too. Like with my inability to pick up social cues and the like. I think everyone has a bit of narcissism in them. I'm referring to Asperger's Syndrome, rather autism—as per the changes made in the Fifth Edition of the *Diagnostic and Statistical Manual of Mental Disorders (DSM-5)*— at least as I've heard, though I remain unsure. I haven't read it. Autism is one of my diagnoses I've collected over the years, yet I don't mention much of it, generally because within the Schizophrenic and affective, or mood spectrum involving about a baker's dozen of Axis I diagnoses per the *DSM-4*—ugh, just that it all makes me quite a rare case. The doctors all love me because I am "the most interesting person" they've ever met, they say. At least my Tourette's has become emotionally secondary these days. As a boy, that was tough, man. But alas, here I stand!

Practice Makes Perfect

After that one, pure, perfect moment, Claudia disappears again. The first day, Georgie wanders around aimlessly, wanting her back. The second day he checks the cupboards and realizes he needs to buy food.

Georgie weakly rolls his cart down the aisle at the grocery store, leaning against the bar and shuffling along. He wonders how Claudia could leave him when he is still so weak.

He could die.

If he died, how would she get her money? She is smart enough to know that.

He smiles. Sure, she's smart enough—smart enough to know that he would get back on his feet, if only to crawl back for more.

Georgie briefly considers dying, if only to prove her wrong.

Then he smiles and tosses a few cans of pineapple rings into his cart.

That would be too easy.

Georgie bumps into Margaret on his way out of the store. Their eyes both widen.

"Georgie!" Margaret says.

Georgie keeps walking, his head twisting as he passes her. "Uh, hey. I'm, uh . . ."

Margaret frowns. "Yeah, sure. See you some other time, then."

Georgie nods. "Later."

And then he's gone.

Claudia places herself softly in the shadow of a street kiosk. The clock on her cell phone reads 2:30 pm. It has been over a day since Georgie last left his house. She knows he will need some smokes soon. She stands in the corner of the kiosk, smoking a slim and watching passersby purchase magazines, cigs, and candy.

Just as she has finished smoking her first slim down to the filter, Georgie approaches the counter. With a grin, Claudia crushes the stub beneath her shiny red sling-backs.

The clerk behind the counter hands Georgie his regular smokes. Without a word, Georgie nods and leaves a fistful of cash on the counter (way more than they are worth), and then turns. Claudia sidles up behind him.

"Fancy meeting you here," she whispers in his ear. She savors a momentary thrill as he stiffens. His quick gasp is music to her.

"Claudia . . ." he breathes. He turns around.

Claudia takes a step back, smiling at him, just out of arm's reach.

"I feel like we're drifting apart," she pouts. "I don't want us to become indifferent to each other."

Georgie grins, knowing her game too well already.

"I'll call you, tomorrow." Claudia smiles and winks at him. Then, with a whiff of perfume and stale cigarette smoke, she drifts back into the shadow of the kiosk, and Georgie is alone in the bright daylight of the street.

The day passes without a call from Claudia. Georgie paces, checking the windows. He sits on his front porch, smoking and watching her house. He builds his 10 shots of espresso and gulps them down until . . .

Night falls and he is a wraith, flitting from one window to the next. For a moment, it appears that a light glimmers deep within Claudia's home. But then he blinks, and it is gone.

The next day, Georgie's alarm blares at the usual time. He slams a hand down on the ever-screeching timepiece. Morning light streams through the white blinds, splashing on his dark and dirty carpet.

When Georgie finally sits up, he blinks. The clock alarm flashes 12:00 pm. Georgie moves the blinds slightly and peers out at Claudia's house. This is now part of his morning ritual—to see if she is home, to see if she came home, to see if she has left home. Not knowing where she is, that is a sweet torture indeed.

Her car is parked out front.

He looks down at his limp dick: soft and sagging between his flat, resting testes.

Then, Georgie does something entirely uncharacteristic.

He gets out of bed.

He staggers through the lonely house. As he walks past the bathroom he decides to turn the shower on as hot as possible. The still-hot coffee, freshly percolated from earlier that morning, speaks to him.

Georgie looks around the wreck of the room—its counters scattered with broken glass and spilled coffee, the floor covered in bits of food and blue mold.

He turns and walks out, past the bathroom, which billows steam from the running shower. With bare feet, he advances to the front door. Steam pours out behind him as he goes.

Georgie stalks across the grass that separates their two homes, not caring that someone might see him violating the unspoken rule about using sidewalks.

She has upset his whole existence. He may as well upset her lawn.

Georgie pounds on the front door of Claudia's house, knowing she is inside. He is tired of the hold she has on him, tired of the games. Ever since that moment with her, after he came back to from the hospital. Ever since that moment of pure ecstasy, of unadulterated orgasm—he wants just her. He wants her with him all the time. This avoidance-torture is bullshite, it's like he is paying her for what she usually does anyway, and, even worse, it no longer gets him quite as high.

"This isn't what I paid for," he snarls, as she opens the door. Her eyes widen in surprise. "I could pay anyone to avoid me. Most people do it for free."

For a moment, Claudia looks frightened. Then she laughs. "Drives you crazy, doesn't it?"

"That's not the point," Georgie mutters.

Claudia shrugs playfully. "I'm making lunch. Would you like to come in?" she says, turning and waving. She walks to the kitchen without waiting for his answer.

Georgie follows a moment later, leaving the front door swinging open behind him.

Claudia's kitchen glows with yellow light; it is clean but cluttered. The smell of fresh food entices Georgie to step further.

The coils of the gas-burning stove glow orange beneath a flat pan, on which Claudia is frying a sandwich.

"Would you like one?" she gestures politely.

Georgie shakes his head.

Claudia shrugs and nudges the sandwich with her index finger. She flips it with a quick flash of fingertips.

Georgie is amazed at her lack of fear. He winces when, a few minutes later, she pushes the sandwich onto a plate.

"Ouch!" she cries softly, as the skin of her finger grazes the hot pan. She sucks on the finger for a moment. Then she pulls it out of her mouth and, looking at it cross-eyed, blows. Her gaze flicks to Georgie for a moment. She smiles.

"Why don't you give it a try?" she says slyly. She points at the pan with her burned finger. "Just a little touch."

With a mixture of dread and elation, Georgie slowly brings his finger close to the hot pan. Searing pain blanks his mind, followed by blissful numbness. He pulls his finger off and runs it under the cold water of her sink. The burn throbs painfully, filling him.

"Owww," he moans quietly.

"Not bad, eh?" Claudia insists.

Georgie nods, sucking on his finger. He looks at Claudia appraisingly, lingering his gaze over her hips and breasts.

"I know," she says finally, grinning. "Why don't you sit on it?"

"What?"

Georgie looks at the hot pan. A final hiss of butter burns with a wisp of smoke from its black surface. He looks back at Claudia, thinking longingly.

"Do it," she says. "Don't make me make you." She glares at him.

With one more wistful glance at Claudia, Georgie eases himself onto the hot pan. It seems only hot at first; it wobbles unsteadily beneath his pudgy bottom. Then, all of a sudden, it scorches him. With a yowl, Georgie leaps from the stove. The pan clangs to the ground behind him. Georgie feels the heat of the burn throb in his backside. He closes his eyes, waiting for the numbness and nothingness of pain to soothe his tormented soul.

"Georgie!" Claudia yells, pointing at the back of his pants. He twists, and realizes that the continued heat was not from the burn, but because his pants are on fire.

"Shite!" he screams. The flames lick up his pants, and threaten to wrap around his belt.

Georgie tugs and jerks at his pants until they crumple to the floor. He leaps away from them.

Given oxygen, the fire leaps higher.

"Jesus, Georgie!" Claudia screams. "Put it out!"

Georgie tries to pick up the burning pants and put them in the sink, but midway through the air the fire scorches his hand.

"Shite!" he yells again, throwing the fireball at the sink. It strikes the wall behind, and flames begin to climb quickly up the drapes.

"Georgie!" Claudia screams. "What are you doing?"

She runs to the pantry and grabs a small fire extinguisher. She stares at the directions on the extinguisher as the fire climbs up the drapes and begins to singe the wallpaper. The nearby cabinets begin to blacken—the laminate melts down in boiling drops that hiss as they land on the stainless steel sink. Claudia struggles with the extinguisher's pin. Unsuccessful, she shoves the extinguisher into Georgie's hands and takes a step away from the burning flames. Georgie looks at the extinguisher, trying to distinguish Step 1 from Step 3. The metal grows warm in his hands as the burning plastic of the laminate cabinets drips heavily onto the counter.

"My ass hurts," he whimpers. He watches as the fire begins to eat away at the wall surrounding the windowsill.

Claudia takes another step backwards, her eyes wide and terrified.

With a squeal, she turns and runs for the front door. Georgie follows fast behind, the extinguisher still tight in his hand.

At the doorway, Claudia suddenly stops and Georgie crashes into her.

"My pictures," she moans, and makes a move to run back inside.

Georgie stops her.

"Call the fire department," he commands, finally abandoning the pain that swelters up and down his thighs and back.

Georgie realizes that he is not wearing any pants. He looks toward the street, where a small crowd of neighbors have gathered.

"What?" he yells at them, then realizes that his underwear is singed, his legs lobster-red. He turns to the street and roars in frustration.

"Call the goddamn police!" he screams, and they scatter.

"My cell phone's inside!" Claudia wails, pulling at her hair. The smoke from the fire has begun to press heavily against her front windows now. Georgie glances at her, pleased with the smudge of smoke on her turned-up nose, and with the frantic, in-drawn terror of her brilliant green eyes. At this moment, he despises her for her idiocy, for her weakness in the face of this catastrophe. At this moment, she is perfect in her inadequacy.

Georgie pulls out the pin from the fire extinguisher with a confident jerk. He throws it on the grass, and scoffs.

"Use my phone," he tells her, pointing at his house.

Without a word, she turns and races for his front door.

Georgie walks into Claudia's burning house and stands in the doorway of the kitchen, watching as the room becomes one huge blaze. He aims the fire extinguisher at the cabinets and begins to spray; watching the white foam as it singes black spots into the fire that ignores it completely.

Like pissing down a well, Georgie thinks, and closes his eyes blissfully.

As the extinguisher runs out, the fire rages on. Georgie takes a step back from the flames, which have only grown hotter. The bulge builds in his shorts. Without warning, his huge cock peeks out between the soft flaps. It thrusts itself forward toward the flames. With a cry, Georgie erupts onto the damage he has caused. The semen spurts in short little gusts, which hiss and boil as they strike the hot floor.

Georgie takes another step back, beaten down by the scorching flames. Seeing there is no hope for the house now, his cum becomes an impossible stream, a pure, lasting orgasm that splashes wetly from the tip of his penis and dissolves into steam in the heat of the fire. Step by slow step, Georgie backs away from the fire, spewing constantly until he reaches the front doorway. The light from the midday sun warms his back, and his dick suddenly sags, lifeless. Georgie staggers backward a few more steps, an idiot grin on his face. With a drooling, gurgling sigh, he collapses backwards onto the lawn.

When the blaring red fire engines finally pull up in front of Claudia's house, flames are flickering teasingly from the attic windows. Claudia is huddled over Georgie, whom she has dragged away from the front of the building after carefully tucking his limp dick back into his shorts.

"My God," he mutters under his breath, his eyelids fluttering rapidly. "My God. Was it good for you?"

Claudia can't help but think that Georgie is delusional.

"Not that great," she mutters. She watches as the firefighters' hoses do nothing against the roaring inferno that was once her home. "Shite. What am I going to do now?" she wonders out loud.

Georgie's eyes open wide. He grins a slow grin.

"You can stay with me," he says quite lucidly. Then he laughs, so quietly, and coughs the last bit of smoke from his lungs.

Dear Diary:

I've got to stop being unhappy with myself. I am perfect. I've got to stop wishing I looked like someone else. I've got to stop hating my body, my face, my personality, and my quirks. I should love them. Without these things, I wouldn't be myself. Why would I want to be someone else? I've got to have confidence in who I am. If anyone hates me for being . . . myself, that's their problem.

I can't let my happiness depend on others. I have to love who I am and be happy. Happiness is simple. Simple is difficult. I guess everybody has their own flaws and imperfections. That's what makes us all special and beautiful. Therefore, to love what it is that makes me different must be the answer because I'm pretty amazing!

Claudia Moves In (Part II)

Claudia skips over to Georgie's California bungalow. Her house is a charred pile, and the insurance company is balking at payment. It's not the first time she has ever moved in with a guy, but it's a step forward in her and Georgie's relationship.

It's not really a relationship, Claudia has to remind herself constantly. It's an arrangement. A purely financial arrangement.

It is only going to last until the insurance money comes through on her house.

But that could take years, Claudia thinks, with a sly nod. Years . . . .

Georgie glances up slowly from his perch on the porch when Claudia crosses the lawn.

She is skipping—actually skipping.

She leaps up the front stairs with a single bound then spreads her arms above her head in a 'V' for victory.

Not bad, for a lady in her 40s, Georgie thinks. This bodes well on the prospects of their sex life.

"It's just until the insurance comes through," Georgie points out. "Nothing to get excited about."

Claudia hangs her head, her mood crushed.

Hey, I thought I was the one supposed to be torturing you, Mr Georgie, she thinks.

She tries out an evil grin, and the look of shock on his face cements her instinct. Lesson number one learned: Never show Georgie your true feelings.

"I'm just thinking of all the fun we're going to have," she says, pouting at him.

Georgie shudders and gives a small smile of anticipation.

Claudia laughs. It was just the reaction she was hoping for.

Asking Claudia to move in was probably the best, and worst, decision of his life. Georgie ponders this epiphany as she plucks the hair from his forearms, one by one, with a pair of tweezers. It was the best decision because now she can't torture him with her absence, which anyone—and everyone—could do. Now, Georgie feels like he is getting what he pays for. And maybe even a little extra.

However, it's the worst decision because he has to see every side of her now. Sometimes she is happy or silly, even though he can tell she tries very hard to be neither of those things when he is watching. Still, no one is perfect. Seeing Claudia in a pleasant mood, in a celebratory mood, kills for Georgie the little sadomasochistic fantasy he is trying to live out with her. It's a buzz kill, is what it is.

Georgie has the chance to examine Claudia from all angles, now. He knows about the tiny wrinkles on the underside of her butt cheeks. He knows about the shining yellow earwax that adorns the outer rim of her ear canal. He knows the yellow glow of the whites of her eyes, and the myriad arteries that grace them.

In short, he knows too much. Much too much.

On the plus side, Georgie gets to torture Claudia a little, too. After all, she is living under his roof. And it is in his nature to do so.

"Hey Claudia, you want to get me a glass of water?" he says lazily one afternoon.

"Do I look like your damn housemaid?" she fires back in reply.

"No . . . although you are on the payroll," Georgie muses. "Unless you'd rather not be?"

Claudia slams shut the book she was reading and stands up. She glares at the back of his head. Georgie is not exactly sure how he knows this, but he does. Claudia stomps into the kitchen, muttering. When she returns, she is holding a tall glass of water. She holds it high above him, presenting it to him like a bottle of wine. Georgie nods, smirking.

With an expression that echoes the contempt of his, Claudia pours the water into his lap.

It is scalding hot. Georgie howls with pain (and pleasure).

"Bitch!" he yells. "Ah . . . !" He sucks air in through his teeth.

Claudia's smile falters slightly. He can see he has an opportunity.

"My balls," Georgie groans. "Damn it . . . I think . . . Ow!" he screeches. "Damnit, Claudia, you burned my nut sack! Shite!" He bends over his crotch protectively.

"Oh God, Georgie—are you okay? I didn't think ". . . ," she sputters.

"Ah. Ah!" Georgie yells. "I might never have an erection again. What if you broke it? Fuck!"

Claudia is crying now, really scared. "Georgie, I didn't know," she sobs. "You've got to believe me. I wouldn't have done it if I knew. God, it was such a stupid, petty thing to do. Stupid. Georgie, I'm so sorry." Tears pour down her cheeks. "Please, please forgive me," she begs him.

"Eh, it's probably nothing," Georgie says simply, and sits back in his chair. He smirks in her direction once again.

Claudia rocks back on her heels, shocked, as she realizes she's been duped.

Lesson number two, she thinks. Never believe a thing that Georgie says.

For days, Claudia mopes around Georgie's house. At first, she was excited to move in with him. Now, there is no excitement left. Just drudgery. For one thing, neither she nor Georgie have a job. The closest thing Claudia has to a job is the perpetual torment of Georgie. This was easy when she could do so by absenting herself. But at this point, living with him, she has nowhere else to go. She has to actually . . . do stuff.

Claudia drifts into the kitchen, which she has managed to scrub to a pleasing, sterile shine. The appliances glint miraculously. Yet, when she opens the refrigerator, all that greets her is ketchup and steak sauce, a pizza box with one dry slice left, three beers in an ancient 12-pack, and a sadomasochistic porno mag.

She picks up the pizza slice, leaving the empty box, and grabs a beer. Thinking twice, she nips the S&M magazine off the middle shelf, thinking it wouldn't hurt to get a few new ideas. Georgie seems pretty tired of the cigarette burning and pinching bit—he may even have left the magazine in the refrigerator for her to find. Or absentmindedly set it down and forgot it. Or, for some unknown reason, decided that porn belongs in the refrigerator. With Georgie, it is impossible to know.

Georgie enters the room just as she is leaving, and they both avoid each other's gaze. For the last several days, they have been floating around like this, pretending to be invisible. It is easier, somehow, easier than reconciling her paycheck with the attachment that would otherwise grow between them.

That has been growing, whether we like it or not.

She slides past him in the doorway, looking down at the molding that lines the hall floor. Keeping her eyes on her toes, she walks up the stairs to the red bedroom that she has made her own. She flops against the red and white gauze canopy bed, enjoying the sense of disorientation and dizziness that comes over her from days and days of nothing stacked together all in a row and begins to gnaw at the pizza.

Claudia flips through the magazine as she tears at the stale pizza with her teeth, looking at the pictures with a combination of loathing and embarrassment. When it comes down to it, the pictures are just funny—she wants to laugh. But when she thinks about actually trying the whip and thumbscrews, it makes her feel a little sick.

She licks the crumbs from her fingers and softens the last bit of dry crust in her throat with a long, cool gulp of beer. She laughs, softly, and tries to blink small tears from her eyes. She chugs half the beer and turns the page.

The face on the man in the next page makes her gasp for a moment, until she realizes that it is not Greg. Not really . . .

"Oh . . . ."

She moans in disappointment. She examines what he is doing, and finally notices the woman in the picture. They are twisted into crazy, deformed shapes—his face is marked with pain, hers crazed with triumph. The blood glistens so moistly on his skin that Claudia can almost hear it drip onto the hard wood floors.

Claudia polishes off the last of the beer, touching the picture lightly with her fingertips. With a flash, she sees herself as the girl in the picture, and Greg below her whimpering in pain and desire. She sees herself standing triumphantly over him . . . with a small moan she presses herself against the pillows, touching herself carefully, a small smile spreads across her face.

When she's done, she tiptoes to the doorway, still naked.

"Georgie."

Claudia's voice is a chime that echoes in Georgie's ears as he rummages through the cupboards to figure out where she hid all the damn coffee cups. He perks up; he percolates.

He moves over to the stairs with two long steps. "Yeah?" he calls.

"Would you come up here, darling?" she says, in a deep, seductive voice.

Georgie shrugs and trudges up the stairs.

"What is it?" he says before he turns into the room. As he takes a step inside, the light goes out. He is plunged into darkness.

Claudia's voice seems to bleed out of the walls. "Just one more step in, Georgie," she coaxes him. "Wait, stop! Now one to your right."

Georgie breaks into a sweat. A low rumble sounds in the darkness before him, seeming to come from the floor.

"Watch out," Claudia purrs. "You don't want to wake it up, do you?"

Georgie feels himself shrinking, but as he is shrinking the walls close in on him—he can't see them but he can feel the air of the room grow tighter, denser. The air wraps around him, trapping him in place. He can't breathe.

"Claudia!" he screams. "Let me out!"

Claudia's laugh echoes from the walls. She is not in the room with him. There is no room.

"Claudia!" Georgie screams. He flails with his arms and strikes hard wood on every side. His wrist tingles where it has struck the wall—his elbow explodes in a series of sparked nerves. He turns back around, beating at the door behind him, which is not a door any more but a wall—not a room but a box, a dark, airless box.

This is my coffin, Georgie realizes, with a terror that chokes him and brings him to his knees. I'm dying, I'm dead; she killed me.

(Who killed you, Ben?

Not me, Dr C, not me . . . .)

Georgie collapses into dark nothingness. His slumping body knocks the side of the coffin, bringing it crashing down to the floor. Georgie lies in it helplessly, in a daze, his fingers twitching feebly against the wood.

When Georgie wakes up, he's in his bed with Claudia. The sheets around him are thrashed, twisted up like a thick rope.

The ones around Claudia are somehow unmoved, as smooth as sand dunes in moonlight.

A dream? He wonders. Or did she wait until I passed out and haul me into bed?

Claudia rolls over, and even asleep the look on her face is triumphant, gloating.

Georgie will never know if it was a dream or not.

(Well, wait, Ben—was it a dream or wasn't it?

How am I supposed to know, Dr C? When I'm Georgie, and he's me—I only know what Georgie knows, and he . . .

Does Georgie know what you know, Ben?

Sheesh, Dr C. Lighten up a bit, will ya? I can't tell you, yet . . . can't tell yet.)

Georgie feels a cold hand wrap around his heart. He rolls himself over and attempts to go back to sleep.

The blue full moon lights up Georgie and Claudia on the white sand beach. They are a happy-go-lucky, fun couple: all white-toothed smiles and sleepy bedroom looks. It's as if though they are posing for cheap promotional brochures for some ritzy beachside resort or spa.

Georgie and Claudia chase each other playfully around the big white sand dune. Claudia dips her feet in the white-foamed seawater as she sits at the edge, where the water mixes with the sand. Georgie tries to lick her wet, gritty feet, but she grinds his face into the salty tidewater, using her perfectly-manicured, stylish feet to hold his head down. Georgie's hair bobs up and down with the rising and falling waves as Claudia laughs.

As the sun sets, Georgie and Claudia dance in the empty beach parking lot, near his sporty gull-winged car. The car's CD player is set on high volume, playing '80s disco music with a pulsing, throbbing beat.

In the background, a silent fire alarm wails.

During the day, Georgie is a zombie. His dreams unsettle, unnerve him. He's terrified they are real, and that he doesn't know it. He is afraid that they are false, and the daytime is what's actually real. He is afraid to sleep, afraid to wake up.

He is fearful he might be going crazy.

Georgie zombies through the kitchen, the living room, the front porch, onto the back stoop, and over again. Sometimes he zombies out on the couch, just staring at the wreck of Claudia's burned-down house.

That must be real, if he can see it, if it's there all the time. That must be real, at least.

Georgie is so out of it that when the house phone rings, he actually answers it for once.

"Geow-gie boy!" his mother's voice cries out joyously over the line. "Lord, I thought I would never hear your voice again! How you been, Geow-gie?"

Of all the times to forget to let the answering machine get it! "Hi, Ma," Georgie mutters.

Claudia, in the next room, pricks up her ears. Georgie can see mischief brewing in her brain, and he makes haste to avoid it.

"Hey, I can't talk right now, Ma," he says. "I'm pretty busy."

"What, ya think you're some kind of big shot, Mr Geow-gie?" his mother teases. "Mr Big Shot don't have time for his own muh-thah?"

Claudia's hand snakes around the side of his head and plucks the receiver from his hands.

"Mrs Gust!" Claudia says pleasantly. "I am so glad you called." Her eyes narrow wickedly.

Georgie can hear his mother asking "And who might you be?"

"I can't say I'm surprised Georgie hasn't mentioned me to you yet," Claudia schmoozes. "He's such a secretive little devil, isn't he?"

Georgie can hear his mother most rapidly assenting, and knows that the battle is lost before he can even begin fighting. His mother will love Claudia. Discussing Georgie's many faults is something she can go on about for hours.

He sits down heavily on the floor and looks up at her, begging her not to do damage she can't undo.

For God's sake, please don't invite us to dinner, he prays.

"I'm Georgie's girlfriend," Claudia reveals. "His live-in girlfriend."

The sound of his mother babbling in disbelief rises so much that Claudia has to hold the receiver away from her ear. She grins wickedly at Georgie.

"I know, Mrs Gust. Georgie's quite the catch." She winks at him. "Yes, yes. *Your* Georgie. Georgie Gust." Claudia nods. "That's the one."

Georgie can make out the sound of his mother inviting them: "Oh, we must have you over for di-nah."

"I'd be so pleased to meet you and your husband. Oh, yes. Georgie is delighted too. Next Thursday? Perfect."

Claudia laughs. "Oh, yes, I'm writing it on the calendar. Next Thursday. I promise. Bye, Mrs G."

With a triumphant smile, Claudia hands the phone back over to Georgie. "She wants to talk to you," she says.

"Geow-gie!" his mother yells at him. "Howdja get such a nice goyil-friend? I can't wait to see you two on Thursday. I love her already!"

A pause.

"She's not one of those vegetarians, is she?"

"Georgie." Claudia's voice is a raspy, raw edged thing that sets Georgie's heart beating. He runs to the stairs, knowing what's to come and wanting it anyway. "Yeah?" he calls.

"Would you come up here, darling?" she says in a deep voice that is not quite her own.

He takes the stairs two at a time.

"What is it?" he says, before he turns into the room.

He sees her.

She's lying on her side, facing the doorway. Naked. She pats the bedspread beside her.

"Just more of the same," she says, with an evil gleam in her eye.

He takes two steps and a hop that lands him on the bed. He grins.

"You just lie back," she commands.

Georgie complies.

With a few deft gestures, she frees his already hard cock from his khakis. A nip of his nipple and a quick, bruising pinch of nails at his pudgy sides, Claudia then lowers her face to his groin.

"Ah . . . all right," he stutters, watching her intently.

She goes down, pulling his shaft up, up inside her mouth. Her tongue is moist and does a little dance around him. He moans as his blood rushes to the very ends of him.

Slowly, Claudia clenches her teeth against him.

"Ah! Ow," Georgie warns her.

She laughs, the sound muffled by his big pussy-spear. She sucks him hard and he moans.

"Oh . . . !"

Then her teeth scrape him again.

"Ow!" Georgie yells.

Claudia swiftly pulls her head up. She glares at him with her glittery green eyes. Shut up," she commands.

He opens his mouth and then snaps it shut.

She sucks him down again and Georgie can feel himself starting to disappear inside of her, down the black tunnel of her throat. She is scraping, scraping him away like a cheese grater, and soon he will be nothing but a tiny little carrot . . . and then a stub . . . and then nothing.

He cries out with terror and pain, but the blood pounds faster and faster into his dick. He feels the pain as a kind of ecstasy. It moves his blood. Everything throbs. The pain and the pleasure. Together. Pounding. Pounding in his ears.

Georgie screams, "Oh God, oh fuck!" as everything rises up in him all at once.

Claudia jerks her head up with one final slash of her teeth. She wipes her mouth and grins.

"What . . . what? No! I'm so close!" Georgie pleads.

Again, she flashes him a wicked, evil grin. "Aww, what a shame," she says, lifting herself off the bed and swiftly pulling her clothes back on. Georgie's dick and balls are screaming at him, throbbing still. He looks down, expecting the whole thing to be in shreds.

Instead it pulses purple at him, an angry tower.

Now even my cock hates me, Georgie thinks, as Claudia gives one last flip of her hair.

At the doorway, she looks over her shoulder for one final gloat. "You didn't think it would be that easy, did you?" she taunts him.

And then she is gone.

Dear Diary:

Life seems to give me answers in three ways. It says, "Yes" and gives whatever we want. It says, "No" and gives me something better. It says, "Wait" and gives me the best. If I'm committed to my dreams, I'll win anyway—to not just dream, but to live our dreams, and to keep moving towards them.

Dinner with the Gusts

"Geow-gie!" Mrs Gust screeches when she opens the door to her son. "Geow-gie, you haven't been over in ages!"

Mama Gust is a huge woman dressed completely in purple spandex. Her hair poofs around her thick jowls like a ball of cotton. One forgotten curler hangs from a lock behind her ear, like jewelry.

When she wraps Georgie in a hug, her body engulfs him, sucking him into the fat rolls of her enormous belly. For a moment, he cannot breathe.

"And Claw-dia!" she yells. Georgie snorts at the accuracy of her misnomer. Claw-dia has claws, all right. "Claw-dia, you're so old!"

Georgie laughs out loud at the look on Claudia's face. It looks like she is about to get a little more than she bargained for.

"Well, I'm sorry, dear, but you must know that Georgie here is only 32." Then Georgie's mother seems to remember what a "lovely goyil" Claudia is. "But who am I to judge?" she concludes. "You two are happy, arentcha?"

Georgie and Claudia nod uncomfortably, without looking at each other.

"Well, that's that, then!" Georgie's mother brushes her hands together and shifts herself out of the doorway so Claudia and Georgie can enter.

The front hall is enormous. It is clear to Claudia that the Gusts have money. A curving marble staircase ascends to her right. A chandelier hangs from the vaulted ceiling, dripping money.

"Your father's at the table," Georgie's mother yells to them as she disappears down a long hall. "Dinner will be out in a minute."

"Not my father!" Georgie mutters, glancing at Claudia. "Not my father, too! You know I can't stand him, Claudia!"

She just shrugs. "I know."

Georgie leads her into the dining room, where they are greeted by another crystal chandelier, a shining dark-wood dining table large enough to seat twelve, and Georgie's father, who rises up from his third martini. The flush in his face and the gleam in his eye gives him dead away.

"Georgie-boy!" he says, a little too loudly. "Georgie-boy, you finally came! And with a girl, too." He appraises Claudia with a knowing eye. "A pretty little thing, isn't she?" he says finally.

"She's in her 40s," Georgie's mother screams from the kitchen. Claudia flinches.

"Now don't listen to her," Georgie's father says in a low voice, taking Claudia by the elbow. "She's just jealous."

He winks and guides her to her place at the table.

Georgie pops open the bottle of wine they have brought for the occasion and serves Claudia, himself, and his mother a glass. Georgie's father declines, gesturing to the martini pitcher on the sideboard.

"Gotta dance with the girl that brung ya," he jokes.

In a few minutes, Georgie's mother sails from the kitchen with a rolling cart packed with food—a glazed ham, scalloped potatoes, asparagus wrapped in prosciutto, tomato slices topped with basil and broiled mozzarella, and a huge bowl of fresh garden salad.

"Well, help yourselves," Georgie's mother cries. "You both look about half-starved."

"Thank you, Mrs Gust. This looks amazing," Claudia says politely, hiding her smile.

Georgie's mother heaps an extra spoonful of potatoes on Claudia's plate. "Oh, I do what I can," she says.

There is only the sound of chewing and the mumbling of appreciative comments for a while. Then:

"So where didja two meet, then?" Georgie's mother asks.

"Oh, we were neighbors," Claudia explains.

"Didn't have too far to move, then, didja?" Georgie's mother jokes.

Georgie and Claudia both nod.

"Hm," Georgie's father mumbles into his ham.

"So Georgie's Tourette's doesn't bother ya, then?" Georgie's mother continues. "It runs most of the goyils off. Then again, with you being so old and all."

"Ma," Georgie whines. "Claudia's not old."

"Well, the goyil knows her age," Georgie's mother says huffily. She turns back to Claudia. "Anyway, we are just so glad that you gave our Geow-gie a chance. He needs a lady around, someone to pick up after him. You take good care of our boy, dontcha Claw-dia?"

Claudia grins. "Of course, Mrs Gust. Georgie's a little rough around the edges, but he cleans up real nice." She reaches over and ruffles his hair.

Both Georgie and his mother stare at the affectionate gesture. Georgie's father snickers slightly.

"The Tourette's isn't catching, you know," Georgie's mother says, continuing on her favorite topic. "You don't need to worry about coming down with it. Though your kids might."

"Ma!" Georgie snaps. The last thing he needs is his mom putting ideas in Claudia's head.

"Ma," he continues, changing the subject, "How is everything down at the club?"

"Oh, same as ever, Geow-gie dear," she says, patting his hand with her own. "Those same bitches always sniffing 'round with their noses in the air, and your father's tennis game is as bad as ever. I don't know why we bother to keep up our membership, Huey, it's so damn expensive."

"Dear, it doesn't matter that it's expensive," Georgie's father says very carefully. "We already have more money than we know what to do with."

Claudia glances over at Georgie to confirm that this is true. His face is still as stone, but she can tell that Georgie knows his father is right. This explains so much. Like why Georgie never seems to worry about not having a job.

"So, Mr and Mrs Gust," Claudia breaks the tension, "where did you two meet?"

"Oh, it was so romantic," Georgie's mother gushes. "We met at the beach, under the moonlight. Do ya remember it, Huey?"

"No, no. We met at the restaurant. Remember?" Georgie's father shakes his head disdainfully and turns to Claudia. "Well, we knew each other in high school, of course. But we met up again at a restaurant here in town."

"Aw, I like the beach story better, Huey," Georgie's mother whines playfully.

"Well, you can't make it more real just because you like it better," Georgie's father snaps.

Claudia and Georgie begin to pay very close attention to the food on their plates.

"Gosh, Huey, don't get so upset," Georgie's mother says in a hushed voice. "We've got company."

Georgie's father mumbles, polishes off his martini, and attends to his potatoes.

"We met at the beach," Georgie's mother continues, as if nothing at all had happened. "At a party. We were so young back then! But even then, I knew that Huey would ask me to marry him . . . someday. Oh, we danced all night"—"

She stops abruptly and looks at Claudia and Georgie. "Do you two go dancing?" she asks. "You really should. Maybe Geow-gie's got two left feet, but you should still go dancing."

Georgie shrugs.

"Maybe sometime," Claudia says.

Georgie's mother nods (once, twice, three times).

Finally, she says, "Are ya ready fer some dessert? I bet yer ready fer some dessert." She stands up and waddles from the room.

Georgie's father helps himself to the martini pitcher on the sideboard, while Claudia tries to catch Georgie's eye. She had come here to humiliate Georgie in front of his family, to torture him with their disapproval and disgust. But she finds that she is too late. They already have plenty of disapproval and disgust with Georgie. They can hardly stand each other, let alone him.

Having dinner with his parents is torture enough for him.

Claudia wonders if there is a way to utilize dinner-with-the-parents torture without her actually having to be there, but she suspects that if she is not there to drag Georgie along, he probably wouldn't go.

She can't really blame him.

"Here it is," Georgie's mother sings out as she comes back through the door. She has a three-tiered cake on a beautiful silver pedestal, blazing with candles. "It's for your birthday, Geow-gie!"

She sets the cake down on the table. The top is decorated with racecars and checkered flags.

"It's not my birthday," Georgie says sullenly. Still, his eyes light up as he looks at the cake. It might just be the glow of the candles, though.

"It's for all the birthdays ya missed having with us," Georgie's mother said. Claudia wonders if the guilt trip is on purpose, but all she can detect in the woman's face is a happy glow.

Georgie's mother exudes guilt. It's not that she tries to make people feel bad, just that her very existence makes people feel bad.

"When Geow-gie was little, he always wanted to be a racecar driver," Georgie's mother explains to Claudia. "Ever since he was little, he wanted to be a driver."

"Who wouldn't?" Claudia exclaims.

When no one is looking, Claudia sneaks one of the candles off the top of the cake. She holds it at an angle under the table, so that the hot wax drips slowly on the crotch of Georgie's pants. She knows it doesn't hurt him, not much at least. It is more like a pact, of sorts. Or a gesture of friendship.

Georgie finds her free hand with one of his and squeezes it, tight. She can see a tiny tear glimmering in the corner of his eye. Then, with a long-suffering sigh, Georgie blows the candles out.

Dear Diary:

Yikes, when someone is just here—or there—for me, it can sometimes bring even just some hope when all else seems completely hopeless. I trudge on.

The Fruits of His Labor

(Isolate me. Destroy me. Tear out my eyeballs and do your dance in the sockets.

You know you love me. I know you hate me. Let's love and hate our way to the bank to the grave to the back of my shiny new car.

Trap me. Smother me. Strangle me into nothingness.

I want your blood and flesh to become apparent to me. I want to meet your hungry, tearing inner ego. There's only one way to go, now, and that is to disappear in your loving strangle, your twisting dark galaxy.

Isolate me. Love me. Destroy me.)

Georgie opens his eyes and realizes that everyone is staring at him. Everyone. Who are these people? Why am I here?

"Don't you remember?" Claudia's voice taunts him. "You wanted this."

Georgie blinks and looks around, not finding Claudia anywhere. Instead, he is surrounded by a wall of faces. They all stare at him, mouths agape.

A child makes a small sound and its mother pulls it close, protecting its face with her hands.

"What . . . ?" Georgie finally croaks.

A man steps out from the crowd.

"Just what do you think you're doing?" the man demands. His voice is angry, though his eyes convey something of an understanding smile.

"I . . . I don't know," Georgie says.

The man's face distorts with mockery, with hatred.

"There's obviously something wrong with him," a woman to his left whispers.

Georgie looks down at himself.

He is naked.

Georgie staggers away from the people, trying to hide himself behind his hands. His face is a ball of fire that ends in bright splashes on his back.

"Fuck," Georgie mutters. "Fuck, fuck, fuck."

He has no idea how he came to be naked in the streets, only the vague sense that it is Claudia's fault.

He doesn't even know where he is. He steps into three different stores before finding someone who will not scream and shove him back out into the street again. Finally, he steps into a dingy corner drug store, which is being watched over by a wrinkled old clerk who has probably seen everything there is to see.

"Can I use your phone?" Georgie asks, desperately, panting. The clerk eyeballs him, from the slight fat rolls of his neck to his thick ankles.

"You better cover up," the clerk says slowly. His face doesn't twitch—not even an inch.

Georgie gapes at the man. He gestures up and down the length and width of his naked body.

"I can't," he squeaks. "I just woke up like this."

The clerk shrugs. He points to the bargain bin in the corner, which overflows with t-shirts.

"Buy a t-shirt. Then you can use the phone," the old man suggests.

"Does it look like I have my wallet on me?" Georgie gestures frantically to his pocket-less, bare legs.

The old clerk raises his eyebrows then points at Georgie's right hand. Georgie lifts his hand and realizes that he has been holding his wallet the entire time.

Really, he wonders.

(What's real, really?)

Georgie pulls out a 10 and buys a t-shirt. It is so long that the cotton falls around his knees. He feels like a little kid in an old-fashioned nightie.

The old man smiles. "Phone's back here," he says, gesturing behind the counter.

Georgie comes around to the back of the counter and feels an instant sense of relief. From behind the counter, his legs are hidden. To anyone on the other side of the counter, he is just a guy wearing a really long t-shirt.

"Hello?" Ben's voice speaks into his ear through the phone.

"Ben," Georgie gasps with relief. "Ben, you gotta to come get me. I'm . . . I'm . . . Claudia . . . Shite, you just have to come get me. Now!"

There is a muffled sound on the other end of the phone. "Sure thing, Mr Gust. Where are you?"

"Uh . . .," Georgie looks around him then lifts his mouth over the top of the receiver. "Hey," he asks the clerk. "Where am I?"

The old man snorts unbelievingly. "Don't ask me," he says.

"What? You don't know where we are?" Georgie exclaims. "It's your store, isn't it?"

"Oh, I know where *I* am," the old man says, a smile tugging the corner of his wrinkled old mouth. "But as for you . . . I thoroughly believe *you* are somewhere else entirely. Yessiree . . . ."

Georgie sighs. "Just the address please," he tells the clerk. "Please."

When Georgie hangs up the phone, the clerk gestures towards the door.

"No pants, no service," he says. "Bad for business."

"But you don't sell any pants," Georgie points out.

The shopkeeper crosses his arms and sighs audibly through his nose.

"What if I stay behind the counter?" Georgie pleads. "No one can tell I'm not wearing pants when I'm back there."

The old man shakes his head. "Last thing I need is a man swinging loose behind my counter," he says gruffly.

Georgie suddenly gets the idea that this might be one of those stores that carries a shotgun somewhere behind the counter. He whisks himself out to the street and leans against the corner of the building, trying to hide in its narrow shadow.

Finally, finally, finally, Ben pulls up in the limo.

When Georgie arrives back at his house, Claudia is reading a book in the living room.

"Did you have a nice time?" she asks, without looking up.

"What d-do you think!" Georgie yells. He gestures to the long t-shirt, which drifts around him like an old-fashioned nightshirt.

Claudia looks at him finally. She snorts.

"Th-this isn't what I wanted!" Georgie wails. He sits down across from her. The shirt rides up to his waist, exposing his balls. They look shriveled and sad, peeking out from beneath the cotton drape.

He doesn't seem to notice. Or if he does, he doesn't seem to care.

"How did you do it?" he asks her.

Claudia points her chin at the bookshelf. One of the books has been pulled from its place and lies face down on the shelf, its binding facing outward.

"*Everyday Hypnotism*," Georgie reads out loud. "Christ . . . ."

With a sinking feeling, Georgie realizes Claudia could do the same thing to him again. Every day, if she wanted. He doesn't even know what the trigger is. The special phrase that'll send him into the streets naked again. There is no way to stop her, to undo what she has done. From this moment onward, Georgie's nakedness is her plaything, her bare plastic doll. She can dance his boys out on the street any time she wants.

The fear of her power over him tightens his gut. This is part of the torture.

"You can't do this kind of stuff," Georgie explains. "What will people think?"

Claudia looks at him steadily. "Since when do you care what people think?"

"C-cunt," Georgie mutters.

"You love it," she insists.

Georgie pulls out his wallet and gives her an extra grand for the month. Although he would never say it out loud, the money is proof enough. She has earned it.

"Where do you come up with this shite?"

Claudia smiles vacantly, her eyes cold and unrevealing. She says nothing.

Shuddering, Georgie turns from her and moves carefully upstairs.

Later that afternoon, Georgie hears the doorbell ring. He doesn't move. Maybe it is the police, to take him in for public exposure. If not this time, sooner or later they will come. The doorbell rings again, and he realizes that Claudia has not answered it. Grudgingly, he trudges downstairs. He can hear voices in the doorway. When he reaches the bottom of the staircase, the door clicks closed. The hall is empty.

(Parenthetical Pet Peeve) Door-to-door salespeople.

Georgie moves to the window that overlooks the front porch. Who is she talking to? Rage and injustice course through him as he considers the thought that Claudia might have struck up acquaintance with an old lover. He peeks carefully between the blinds.

She is talking to a woman, whose back is to Georgie.

"I just wanted to make sure he's okay," the woman says. The voice is Margaret's. Georgie's heart skips a beat. "A friend of mine saw him downtown earlier today."

"He's fine," Claudia says, with a slippery smile. The afternoon sun slides across her cheek. "Really. I mean, of course he's embarrassed about it, but he's taking the whole thing awfully well."

Margaret sits down on a wicker chair, turning so Georgie can see her face. She frowns. "I just don't understand how it could have happened. It's not the sort of thing that happens by accident."

Claudia looks at Margaret with something close to pity. "Georgie has issues, Margaret," she says. "You can't just take a person to meet the Dalai Lama and assume he'll be magically healed."

"Then he's not doing 'awfully well,' is he?" Margaret says heatedly.

Claudia cuts her off with a gesture. "He's seeing someone. It's being taken care of."

"Well, I . . . I just want to make sure he's okay, that's all," Margaret stutters.

"Of course you do," Claudia sniffs. "You spend two weeks 'nursing' him back to health in an exotic location and the second you get back you abandon him. You want to make sure that he's okay, only as long as that means that you don't have to do anything."

Georgie feels a pang in his stomach as he watches Margaret's face twitch with guilt. He wants to yell: "Don't hurt my friend!" But he doesn't. He just keeps watching.

"I . . . I," Margaret stutters.

"You have no stake in his future anymore," Claudia insists. "I'm taking care of Georgie now. Full time."

Claudia stretches herself up tall, and Georgie is amazed by how imposing she is.

Margaret's face fills with a suppressed panic. "Oh?" she says creakily. Then she seems to find some strength in herself. "Well, then, I can only hope he's in good hands," she says, then flees the porch before Claudia can say another word.

At the sight of Margaret's small figure turning swiftly up the street, Georgie feels the dark knot inside of him grow bigger. Margaret . . . he thinks. But he can't quite finish the thought.

Claudia turns back toward the house, a satisfied smirk curling her lips. She notices Georgie peeking out at her from the blinds and laughs. Georgie looks up at her in horror.

"She's my friend!" Georgie yells at her through the window.

She frowns for only a second. Then she mocks him, her voice muffled by the glass.

(Parenthetical Pet Peeve) Grown women with voices like a 6-year-old. "Aw, poor Georgie. Your friends don't like you anymore, is that it?" she says in a sing-song voice.

He gapes at her.

She steps inside the front door. "It's your own damn fault," she hisses, her face coming close to his.

The sad truth is she's right. Georgie sinks into the despair that is clamoring inside him, trying to find peace in numbness. Instead, he finds only turmoil and fear. The misery is part of the torture, he reminds himself. But still he finds it difficult to believe. This is not what I wanted, something insists.

(Yes, it is.)

"You're so pathetic," Claudia continues. She can see that he is sinking, but wants to plunge him under. "You care so much about what other people think that it even makes you look desperate."

The well-trained Georgie tries to argue. "No, I'm an individual!" But the secret, drowning Georgie knows that what she is saying is true. He despises himself.

"You're so pathetic. You beg for love and attention, but don't even know how to get it," Claudia continues. "You're such an idiot, hopping around in that silly blue hat, moping after your cigarettes like a fucking zombie. If you want people to like you, why don't you just act like a normal person?"

Georgie tries to straighten up as an overwhelming rage builds in him.

"F-f-f . . . f-f-fuck you!" he shouts.

He charges out the front door, turning up the street in the direction where Margaret went. She is nowhere to be seen, but he keeps walking anyway.

Dear Diary:

Just a thought of the day—always be willing to change!

It's All in a Day's Work

Claudia dreams that she is having dinner with the Gusts. Except that instead of a ham, there is an entire roasted pig on the table, an apple shoved in its snout. And there are tall, slim candles lighting the dark wood table, dripping rivulets of wax. Wasted wax, Claudia thinks in the dream.

Georgie's mother comes to the table with a pair of thick, round goggles over her eyes and a leather helmet on her head. She sits. "Geow-gie always wanted to be a driver," she says.

"Ma!" Georgie whines. In Claudia's dream, he is only five years old, although everyone treats him like he is 30.

"Georgie and I are lovers!" Claudia blurts out. Everyone looks up at her. Now she's done it.

"Well, why wouldntcha be, dear?" Georgie's mother asks, dishing out more potatoes.

Through the dream, Claudia realizes that Georgie is not married. He is not Greg. She can't hurt Georgie in the same way that she wants to hurt Greg. And hurting Georgie will not hurt Greg—not one bit.

Claudia wakes up from the dream filled with an aching sense of loss. For some reason, she can't say why, it feels like someone she loved very dearly has just died.

"Georgie," Claudia says quietly, kindly, one evening.

He looks up at her in surprise. Her eyes are wide, her expression innocent and caring. Georgie feels a sudden certainty that everything they have been through in the last few months has just been a dream. He will wake up any minute and discover that they are actually happy together, and considerate—the American Dream couple, on the outside and in. Maybe they will go for a drive in his shiny black car and dance together on the beach. He is surprised at the sudden bliss this thought gives him, that a satisfying, loving relationship with Claudia is the dream. The nightmare is the reality. He realizes that the bliss between the moments of torture—just an accidental current of happiness—is what makes up his orgasm now. His life is just one torturous sexual act interspersed with brief spurts of joy and relief from pain.

"I was thinking," Claudia continues, looking on him with eyes filled with adoration—maybe false adoration, but Georgia will take it, "what if we went out for dinner tonight?"" You know, like, an actual date?" Her voice sinks down to a whisper. "Like real couples do."

Georgie wonders again if the whole arrangement is a lie. His mind could have created all the torment during an episode, a way to explain all the pain of their normally loving relationship.

But that is impossible.

(Is it, Ben? Is it really?)

"Y-yeah. Sure," he stutters, looking up at her with hope.

"Wonderful." Claudia seems to glow. She drops down and plants a lingering kiss on his forehead. "I have to take a shower. Shouldn't we look nice?"

Georgie can only nod in silence.

Georgie and Claudia step out of his shiny black sedan in front of the neighborhood's premier Italian restaurant. Claudia is dressed to the nines in a slinky green dress that shimmers with her eyes. Her hair falls in soft, red waves down her back. Georgie wears a dark gray suit with pale blue pinstripes. They glide together to the front door of the restaurant. A doorman in a tuxedo opens it as they arrive.

"Georgie, it's beautiful," Claudia says in a hushed tone, as they enter the dining room. It is dimly lit, but filled with mirrors, lighted candles, and glinting crystal. The two are seated in red leather chairs in a corner near the window, where the glow of nearby shops lights their faces.

"Thank you, Georgie," Claudia says, after a sip of water. Her eyes seem to shine. Almost, almost, Georgie convinces himself that their arrangement is a lie, that this momentary connection and consideration are truth. Almost.

Their conversation is light and pleasant, without any bitterness or mention of what has passed between them in the last weeks. Claudia's face seems to glow in the candlelight. Her freckles have all but disappeared. When Georgie squints, he decides that Claudia's hair looks almost like Margaret's.

Their waitress is attractive, tall, and graceful. Her eyes shine, too, as she meets Georgie's gaze. His momentary happiness overflows, and he smiles at her radiantly. He includes Claudia in his smile, feeling suddenly like the three of them wholly understand each other, that the world is at peace and that they are at one with themselves and with the universe.

When the waitress glides off, Georgie sets his hand on the table, halfway between himself and Claudia. He beckons her with his fingers.

"This was a good idea," he says.

"I can't believe you," she hisses.

"What?" Georgie frowns. For a moment, he disbelieves his ears. But her face is a horrible sight, despite the hours she spent making it up. It is twisted into some horrible snarl, an evil mask. She looks like a demon, a gargoyle. "What do you mean?"

He tries desperately to hang on to his earlier happiness.

"I saw how you were acting with the waitress," she says. "Do you think I'm blind?"

She's insane, Georgie realizes, in a moment of inspiration. Completely nuts.

"What are you talking about?" Georgie replies, his voice rising slightly.

"You know what I'm talking about. You were flirting with her," Claudia says, accusingly. An older couple at the next table looks at them disapprovingly.

"I was not," Georgie says. "I didn't say anything."

"Like you need to speak." Claudia scoffs. "You, of all people, should know that you're more attractive when you keep your mouth shut."

"W-where do you . . . how . . . Christ, Claudia! We are at one of the nicest restaurants in town and all you can do is insult me."

"Don't change the subject," she insists. "You were flirting with that girl. She's young enough to be your daughter."

Fellow patrons are becoming tense at Georgie and Claudia's display. Some of them stare at Georgie openly, hostility etched on their face.

"She's young enough to be your daughter," Claudia repeats.

One of the women at the table nearby gasps. She glares at Georgie then stares pityingly at Claudia.

"Men are scum," the woman mutters to her companion, who nods.

"I can't believe you," Claudia says a little louder. "All I want is to have a nice dinner with you . . . ."

"That's what I want, too," Georgie interrupts.

"And all you can do is ogle the waitress." Claudia barrels forward like a freight train. "You disgust me."

At that moment, the waitress brings their food, and Georgie no longer cares about Claudia's disgust. Instead, he stares unflinchingly at the woman's breasts. She seems nice, he thinks to himself. When he turns to his dinner, Claudia slaps him hard across the face.

"You're embarrassing me," she screams. "I spent hours trying to look beautiful for you and in front of all these people you just ignore me and stare at that girl like you're at Hooters or something!"

"These people wouldn't have a clue about it if you weren't yelling so loud," Georgie roars back, losing his temper.

"So you admit it. You were flirting with her," Claudia screeches, triumphant.

"So what if I was?" Georgie returns. "What's the big fucking deal?"

The woman at the nearby table looks sharply at him and he returns her glare. "What the fuck are you looking at?" he snaps.

"You're always doing this to me," Claudia yells. "You have no respect for me or for any woman."

She turns to the sympathetic woman nearby. "He walks around naked, you know," she reveals. "Downtown. It's disgusting."

The woman gasps. "That was him?" she murmurs. She whispers something to her partner. With a glare, they both stand up and leave.

"Sexist," one of the women hisses as they pass.

"Bitch," Georgie mutters. He looks down at his food, his appetite gone.

"You really are something else," Claudia starts in on him again. "What does she have that's so great, huh?"

Georgie rolls his eyes. "Nothing, Claudia. You're perfect just the way you are."

She grunts, unsure what to make of his sarcasm.

"Can we just eat?" Georgie asks, poking at his food with a fork.

"That's all you think about," Claudia says, slamming her napkin down on the table. "Your stomach . . . and your dick."

Bumping the table with her hip as she stands, Claudia glowers down at him. Then, she walks out of the restaurant, leaving Georgie alone in front of two lukewarm plates of food.

Claudia scurries down to the car, her heels clacking against the sidewalk. The secret to Claudia's fake-outs is that they're not really fake. There is a small, secret Claudia inside her, who's actually kind of pissed about the way Georgie and the waitress seemed to have a special moment back there. She doesn't think about the fact that she was included in that moment, too. If she did, it probably wouldn't help Georgie's case, anyway.

A second after she slides her feet across the smooth carpet of Georgie's shiny black car, she doesn't give a shite about the waitress or about Georgie anymore. Or so she tells herself. Instead, she laughs a quiet chuckle and leans back against the seat. She rolls down the divider that separates her from the driver.

"Hey, Ben," she says, her voice throaty and seductive. "How about a drink?"

When Georgie comes home, the lights in the house are blazing. Music plays loudly over the wireless sound system. Claudia is nowhere to be seen. Georgie briefly wonders what horrors are in store for him now. He wonders if an apology would stave off the torture. An apology would be more likely to cause pain, he decides. Claudia would use the moment of weakness to shred his heart.

He pays the bills, after all. What does he need to apologize for?

Georgie stands indecisively in his own front entryway. He could turn around and leave. He could run away, and she would never find him. The Galapagos are nice, this time of year. Any time of year. Maybe he should do it. She can have the house as long as he is free of what is in it.

(He won't.)

Even if I did run away, Georgie thinks, there would be someone else, someone else like her to torture me. There's always a Claudia, no matter what I call her. In that case, Georgie would not be in control. The torture would be part of the love–hate relationship that he is doomed to always repeat. But with Claudia, at least, Georgie is in control. After all, she is only doing what she does because he pays her to.

Georgie fingers his wallet, wondering if he could pay her to stop.

He is afraid of that question, afraid of the answer.

He goes upstairs.

On the covers of his neatly made-by-Claudia bed, Georgie finds a note.

Dearest Georgie, (the note reads)

My dismay at your behavior at dinner this evening, and my own, can know no bounds. You and I have hurt each other so many times that there is nothing left for us to do. It is obvious, as well, that your affection for me has dwindled, and there can be no reviving it. What else is there for me but despair? You are my shelter and my sustenance. I should so much rather lose my life than my heart.

Remember me fondly.

Love ever,

Claudia

Georgie's mind whirls and he considers the note. What does it mean? Has she left him for good? At once his stomach sinks into his groin and his brain rips free of his skull. His thoughts float happily for a second when he thinks about life without Claudia's torture. He feels himself becoming aroused at the thought, all his past rationalizations, for a moment, far behind him.

Then he looks at the note once more, and is filled with terror. Has she? Could she? He races to the bathroom.

She lies within the flame, on the still-cold tile in a pool of blood. The fire, it's happening again. Her arms are sticky with the plasma and platelets; her eyes are glassy and horror-filled. Georgie drops to his knees. He dreams without sleeping.

In Georgie's dream, Claudia's slumped against the counter, and as dreamscapes change, the counter blends and transforms. She's in the kitchen, flooding, too. And the entire kitchen counter's contents, from leftover coffee mugs filled with black coffee bean soot, to the salt and pepper containers, mostly salt.

Salt is the omen of discordance, everything having gone awry with quarrels and discontent. Georgie and Claudia adore salt, they're addicted to love and salt. Everything falls down and apart, slipping and falling over and over back to the bathroom and back to everywhere and nowhere, just like the completely awry love and salt of Georgie and Claudia's discordant relationship.

The kitchen sink water pours like a river, flooding the room—all of the rooms—into a saltwater ocean. Claudia remains on the floor and still in the kitchen. Her kitchen. She falls again, gets up, and falls again, over and over, just like Georgie, freely under the influence of gravity, together they blend into yet another overlapping dream. This entangled and intertwined nightmare, together. The wasted wax, the jealousy, and now the remembrance of Claudia's house fire storms into their combined dream.

Georgie's perspective nearly wakes him. He's lucid now, and can telepathically control this mutual dream, controlling something for once, and once for the benefit of himself, not Claudia. He flickers flashbacks of her house fire. She's burnt. Georgie lights up her middle brain, the place where dreams take place—the emotions, in particular. The sea of saltwater Georgie has created as God said, "Let there be water," as Georgie seems to know, though God wanted an expanse between waters, Georgie just wanted water. All the water coats Claudia's blackened, charred skin, as she remembers, as if she had been inside her own burning home. Fear, lots of fear and discontent, exacerbates the still-sparking hair dryer. It rests just beside her fingertips.

Blending back to the bathroom, Claudia's face is bloated soaked and strange, her hands limp at her sides, her toes pointed down just an inch from the lid of the toilet seat. Georgie rises from his knees. The fire and flood stops dead.

Claudia lay in the bathtub with a broken heart, her arms limp over her face, white and empty against the still water. A nearly empty prescription bottle holds a few white pills. Georgie drops to his knees again. Nobody dreams. They're both wide awake, now, with mere distorted memories as dreams do upon awakening at last.

"Claudia!"

Georgie's voice makes a gargling sound; his tongue seems trapped in his throat. His thoughts are filled with horror, his heart a bleak, terrified thing, and yet the hope, the small hope that now she has disappeared forever tugs softly at him.

"Claudia!"

He feels her slippery hand and finds a pulse. The hope disappears in a cloud of impossibility and guilt. Georgie slaps her across the face. The dreams that were have become real.

"Jesus, Georgie," she yells, sitting bolt upright. "I'm not really dying, you dolt. There was no dream. It's all real, Georgie. What's wrong with you? What in the hell is wrong with you?

She rubs her face with her hand.

"Ow. Sheesh," she says, "Look at what you've done. Look what you've created!"

Georgie gapes at her like a fish. "But . . . the pills . . . the note . . .," he babbles.

Claudia sinks back in to the tub and smiles lazily. She lifts a glass of wine from the rim and brings it to her lips.

"You really think I'd give up all this?" she says finally.

"But what about the waitress? Our date?"

The so-called reality sinks in. Georgie's in la-la land.

"What the hell do I care if you flirt with the waitress or if you don't?" Claudia says with a wave of her hand. She closes her eyes. "I don't kid myself that I have any hold on you."

"Yeah?" Georgie looks at her unflinching face. He tests the waters. "I guess you don't have a hold on me," he says thoughtfully.

He hopes it hurts her. Even if it doesn't hurt her, he is glad to say it out loud. If only to show that he doesn't give a shite, either.

As Georgie leaves her there, he thinks—for just a moment—that he hears her sob. But as he looks back into the tub, Claudia's face is pure, serene, calm. He decides that it was just his imagination, that's all, la-la land or not. It's his damned imagination. It always is. Moonshine penetrates through the window. Beddy-bye time and time to wake up.

Awakened the next morning, all he sees is darkness, darkness again, this time literally. He blinks for a moment, waiting for his eyes to adjust. But there is no light. None at all. Before him is only a vast wall of blackness. Georgie pushes his hands up before his face and sits up straight, adrenaline coursing through him. He cries out.

One hand brushes against soft cloth, the other clutches the matted substance to his side. He is sitting on carpet. He stands and hits his head on something hard, which vibrates with a soft dong when he strikes it. Where am I? Georgie thinks wildly. Is this hell? Am I dead?

"Claudia," he screams.

The light switches on. He is in the closet.

"Sheesh, Georgie," Claudia says, rubbing her eyes. She is wearing her pajamas. "What are you doing in the closet?"

Georgie shakes his head.

Claudia shrugs. "Can you hand me my robe?"

Without a word, he hands it to her. Claudia closes the door. After a moment, she turns out the light. Georgie sits on the floor in the closet, staring into the darkness. It is quiet, and still. A night with no stars, no moon to confuse it. It is a new kind of nothingness. He likes it all right. He is the dreamer who doesn't sleep and the sleeper who never dreams.

Georgie walks down to the kitchen. Claudia is huddled over the coffee-maker, making small noises. Her shoulders are shaking a little.

Georgie wonders if she is crying. Again? What does she have to be sad about, anyway? She is not the one who has to undergo daily torture. Georgie scoffs softly and Claudia straightens up.

"You put me in the closet?" he says grumpily, grabbing a coffee cup.

Claudia sends him a withering glare. Georgie wonders for a moment whether he has begun sleepwalking or if it was just another one of Claudia's hypnosis tricks. Judging from Claudia's face, he figures that he will never know. He decides to laugh.

"That was pretty stupid," he tells her. "I mean, the closet? It's not like I'm claustrophobic or anything."

Claudia shrugs. "Yeah, you sounded pretty calm and collected when you were thrashing around in there," she says sarcastically.

"Hmm," Georgie mutters. He pours himself a cup of coffee and stares at her. He remembers the nothingness of the closet. It was not orgasmic, but it was peaceful. It was all right, he thinks.

(Define "all right," Ben.

You're supposed to be the doctor, Dr C. You tell me.)

"I'm tired of the way you've been treating me," Georgie says. "Last night, this morning. I mean, can't you let up even a little?"

Claudia stares at him. "You don't pay me to let up," she says finally. "I don't even get weekends."

"So am I supposed to feel sorry for you? You're the one who's torturing me. You've done the most despicable things to me, isolated me from my friends. I can't even trust myself right now. I never even know where I'm going to wake up, anymore."

Georgie realizes he is screaming.

"What do you want me to do, Georgie?" Claudia screams back. He is shocked to find that tears are streaming down her face. Her face is shining red and mottled like a cherry. "I'm just doing my job. Now you're telling me I can't even do that right?"

Georgie squirms under her despair.

"It's just that I'm doing it all too well," Claudia accuses him. "You can't handle it, is that it? How is it my fault if you can't make up your mind?"

He can't believe the storm that he has unleashed.

"You can't ask me to do something and then bitch at me when I do it," Claudia screams. "You can't have it both ways, Georgie."

"I can have it any way I want," Georgie insists meanly, irrationally. "I'm the one who's paying you."

Claudia stares at him for half a second then bursts into fresh tears.

"You are so cruel," she sobs.

"Oh, shut up," Georgie says, tired of the guilt trip, not believing her tears are genuine. "You love it. You know you do."

Claudia buries her face in her hands. The sound of her crying fills the kitchen, the whole house.

Georgie can't handle her misery. He leaves.

"I need a smoke," he mutters to himself, slamming the door behind him.

Dear Diary:

The truth is the truth—the present is the present.

Calling for Reinforcements

Georgie wanders up and down the aisles of the grocery store, a pack of cigarettes and a small sack of limes in his hand. He watches the shelves of goods slide past him. Red, green, yellow colored labels. It's a rainbow, Georgie thinks. A rainbow. He stands for a moment, staring dumbly at a can of fried onions.

"Georgie," Margaret calls. "Georgie, over here!"

When Georgie hears her voice, something in him lifts. He turns to see her waving from the end of the aisle.

"I stopped by your house the other day, but . . ." Margaret pauses.

"I wasn't feeling well," Georgie supplies.

"I heard about, um, what happened. Downtown . . . ."

"Yes, that?" Georgie pauses, rubbing his chin meaningfully. "That was embarrassing, wasn't it? Well, I've just had some trouble sleeping, lately. Actually, I've been sleepwalking, Margaret. That's what it was."

Pleased with this fabrication, Georgie asks Margaret how she's been.

"Oh fine, fine," she says, smiling. "Work, you know. Well, I signed my first book deal. I guess you wouldn't have heard about that though, right?"

"That's great," Georgie exclaims with a big smile, wondering since when Margaret wrote.

"What is the book about?" he says finally.

Margaret looks confused for a moment. "Oh my God, I never told you about it?" Margaret beams. "I wrote it years ago, and I've have been submitting it for publication. I had all but given up, but it was finally accepted," she says. "It's about, well, it's about a girl, like me, but with Tourette's and schizophrenia, and well, things get really bad for her, one thing after another, you know. And then she meets a man who can support her, who has the time to care for her, and the money, too."

"Well, that's just great." Georgie's smile is frozen on his face. "Really. What a great story."

"Thank you Georgie." Margaret smiles. "So, uh . . . I met your girlfriend the other day, when I came to meet you?" She says it like a question, like she is not sure whether Claudia is his girlfriend or not.

"Yes, Claudia," Georgie says. "She's just great, isn't she?"

Margaret starts. "Oh yeah," she mumbles. "So, you guys are really happy, huh?"

"You bet." Georgie grins. He is playing the part of a lifetime. "She's like, my soul mate. She's so thoughtful all the time. Really takes care of me, you know?"

Every word pierces her heart. She actually flinches.

"Well, as long as you're happy," she says.

"Oh, I am," Georgie assures her.

His utter bliss gives her no room for doubt; she puts on her happy face, and the mask is complete.

"Well, all right, Georgie. Make sure you tell her that I'm glad she's taking such good care of you." Margaret pauses a moment, and a light flashes in her mind: "Did you get in touch with your nanny, yet?"

"What?" Georgie looks at her blankly.

"Your nanny. The one who used to . . . you know. I thought you were going to confront her?"

"Oh, yeah," Georgie says. "Well, no, I haven't found her yet. She's really hard to find, you know?"

She can tell that Georgie's lying, but drops it for now. She places her hand lightly on his arm. "I'm glad that we're still friends," she says, smiling up at him.

He smiles back with real pleasure. "It sucks to hold a grudge, doesn't it?" he says.

She nods. "If you need anything . . . anything at all," she says quietly, "well, you know you can count on me."

And with that, she turns and rolls her cart down the next aisle without a backward glance.

Georgie knows that Margaret doesn't buy his story about Claudia and his everlasting bliss. But he would not have it any other way. What is the point of being miserable if everyone knows about it?

The house is rocking when Georgie gets back from the store. The windows are blazing light, with only shadows of the people who crowd his living room. Music booms from the windows and walls; the frame seems to shake and creak from the sound waves.

Someone yells at him from his own porch, "Hey, buddy!"

Georgie sneers at the man.

"Sheesh, what's his problem," the man snickers. "Hey, who the hell invited you, anyway?" he yells at Georgie's back.

Georgie slams through the open front door and bumps into a teenaged-looking partygoer on her way out to the porch. She smiles up at him drunkenly, her eyes shining with bright blue makeup.

"Hey, you got a light?" she giggles. "I need a smokes." She laughs again and looks over her shoulder at no one. "Did you hear that? A smokes?"

She takes one look at Georgie's face and then slides past him, bumping arms with the man on the porch. "A smokes!" she snickers, and he laughs loudly with her, dropping an arm lightly on her shoulders.

Ordinarily, Georgie would be all over this party. He would be its wildest fiend.

"Hey, party," he would mumble drunkenly, punctuating the air with a pack of smokes. "Hey, party, you ain't seen nothing yet."

But not here, not in his own little sanctuary, the cave that he has made for himself (and Claudia). Oh no. Instead he is angry, crazy mad; he wants to go ballistic on Claudia, smack her around a little, something–anything. Strange alcoholics and druggies have invaded his untidy little world. Some are knocking over the stacks in the living room; others are raiding the almost empty refrigerator for mayonnaise scrapings and a last warty pickle. Worst of all, with all the people, he can't even find Claudia.

"Fucking bitch," he mutters.

Georgie walks into the kitchen, where there is a blender whirring in the corner. He wonders if it's his blender. Does he even have a blender?

The man at the controls takes his hand off the top for a moment to grab the belt loop of a pretty little blonde standing next to him. With a triumphant rush, the contents of the blender free themselves, sending an explosion of orange liquid and crushed ice all over the counters and floor.

Georgie gapes at the mess, the orgasmic spurt of alcohol that has tainted his otherwise sterile environment.

"Don't worry, man." The guy who took his hand off the top leans his face close to the blonde, although he is talking to Georgie. He fingers a lock of her hair, basks in her willing smile. "I'll take care of it. First thing tomorrow."

Then he addresses the girl like no one else is even there. "Shots?" he suggests.

Georgie stomps out into the back yard, where a crowd of 20- and 30-something men and women dance together to the blaring of music from a fat set of speakers. The crowd gyrates, crooning and moaning together. The muscle heads have all taken their shirts off, and so have some of the skinnier girls. One girl, her waist a long, slender board, wanders around in nothing but a purple lace bra and matching panties—bouncing from chest to chest as she tries to dance.

It is like one big orgy in Georgie's backyard, reminding him of the fetish houses where he used to play.

Except the people at this party are almost all, without exception, remarkably attractive. Georgie sees a flash of red. Curly, wild, orangey-red.

Claudia!

He weaves his way through the bodies, bumping elbows and pushing past the naked flesh of the pulsing, sweating dancers. The stench of collective body odor shoves its way up his nostrils. He tries hard not to gag.

The dancers part a minute and he sees Claudia wedged between two well-muscled young men and doing a good job on both of them. Neither of the men can take their eyes off her, and Georgie can hardly blame them. She is wearing her most fetching black leather halter, her tightest and lowest-cut black leather pants. A shimmering red thong pokes up from her ass crack.

Claudia sees Georgie and winks at him. She flicks the whip she is holding in her right hand so that it curves gently around the cheek of the young man who rides her belly button.

"It's a party, Georgie," she cries drunkenly, flinging her head back. Her hair rises above her face, swirling like flame. "I threw you a party."

"I didn't want a fucking party, Claudia," he yells, grabbing at her elbow. Her eyes open wide, like she is surprised by his anger. He tries to pull her away from the two hunky young men and out of the pumping, thrusting crowd, but one of the men steps in front of him.

"Give the lady some respect," the man says. He crosses his arms over his ridiculously bulging pectorals.

"Yeah," the other man chimes in. He is stockier than the first and still bigger than Georgie.

"Hey, guys," Claudia laughs, trying to lighten the mood. "Let's just dance, huh?"

With one last glower, the two boys turn back to their sexy cougar and resume their half-frenzied attempts to fuck her leather-bound ass.

They will probably both do it, too, once the sun goes down.

Georgie pictures the two of them riding his Claudia, their sweaty and strong young bodies working in tandem with her, forming a cage of flesh around his Claudia . . . . Jealousy twists through his heart like a thick, rusty wire, shoving in deeper than he knew existed.

Why does she bother with me if she can get that? Georgie revels in disgust and self-hatred. Because you're paying her to, dumbass, is the obvious reply. And that brings along a whole new brand of pain.

Georgie thuds noisily up the stairs. In the bedroom, some black-haired bimbo is giving a surfer dude a back massage in Georgie's bed.

"Get the hell out," he yells, and they scram.

"Christ," he mumbles, climbing into the bed with his shoes on. In 10 minutes, he is asleep.

When Georgie sleeps, he dreams of the deep dark of the closet. The silence and peace, the strange anonymity of blackness, soothe his rattled nerves. My dear, my deepest love, your peace is music to my senses. Come and be nothing with me, sink into the bliss of blackness, of a world without us. When Georgie dreams, Claudia is his slave. He strings her up until she is hanging from the ceiling—her wrists chafing from the rope.

"Georgie, please," she screams, terrified. She is not paying him to torture her, after all. He is just doing it for fun.

"Please, Georgie. Just let me down."

"Who's Georgie?" he answers, then laughs. "There's no Georgie here."

Georgie sharpens a knife carefully as he watches her swing. Her eyes saw back and forth with every swipe of the blade.

"Georgie, I couldn't help it," she gasps. "You made me do it. You wanted me to. I just did what you wanted me to do."

Georgie takes the tip of the knife and embeds it into her calf. She screams.

"You wanted to do it," he says finally. "I may have asked you for it, but you wanted to do it."

He slowly drags the blade down to her ankle. He has to tug on it when he gets towards the bottom. Then he slices her Achilles' tendon, psycho-style.

Georgie gets nothing from Claudia now but a series of screams and weeping. "No, no, no, no," she moans, sobbing between cuts.

"How could you do it? How could you know how far to go? How can you know when to stop if you don't know what it's like, Claudia?" he argues with her. He grabs each side of the cut with his fingers and begins to tear the skin away from the muscle, tearing slowly from the back of the calf all the way to her shinbone.

Claudia's screams are a constant, never ending nightmare of pain.

"Shhhh," Georgie soothes her as he gives the skin one last tug, ripping it from her leg. Blood drains from her and pools on the floor.

"This is for your own good," Georgie soothes her.

Then he starts to work on her other leg.

When Georgie comes back to reality *(reality?)*, it is in the strange half-darkness of morning. A searing pain in his arm brings him full awake. Georgie tries to sit up, but a heavy weight holds him down.

Claudia straddles him, naked. She grins fanatically, her hair a glowing orange halo.

"Good morning, lover," she murmurs. Then she slashes at him again with a razor blade, in the chest this time.

"Ow," Georgie cries. But as the blood seeps from the cut, the exclamation turns to a low moan. The numbness and nothingness of this pure, blessed pain is all that he has missed and more.

"Again," he begs.

Georgie doesn't hear the Mexican cleaning crew when they arrive. But they can hear him. They stand uncertainly on the front porch as his voice drifts down from the upstairs window. Georgie is moaning and groaning. Sanchez looks over at Rueben, gives him a swift shrug.

"Sounds like fun, hey?" he mutters.

Rueben just grunts.

"Hey, Maria, why don't you get the coffee started?" Sanchez suggests. He tosses her the keys.

She stares up at the upstairs window with eyes large in fear.

"*Por favor*," she whispers.

Sanchez gives her no pardon. With trembling fingers, she puts the key in the lock. She enters the house of pain, which echoes with Georgie's cries. Then the door closes behind her, and Rueben and Sanchez each light a cigarette, occasionally glancing upward and snickering.

Margaret stands uncertainly at the threshold of Georgie's house. The door is slightly ajar. Inside, the sounds of thumping and knocking echo, along with whispered words in Spanish. More worrisome are the sounds of screaming and moaning from upstairs.

Sanchez pauses when he sees her. A mop is in one hand and a bucket filled with cleaning supplies is in the other.

"Excuse me," he says finally. She moves away from the door to let him through. "Just cleaning up?" she asks as Rueben passes by, closely followed by Maria, who keeps her head down. She is shy.

"Oh, yeah," Rueben whistles through his teeth. "What a riot in there last night, hey?" he winks at Margaret. "Not so quiet this morning, either."

Margaret returns his attitude with a cold smile, and he shrugs boyishly. Then Rueben, Sanchez, and Maria load up the van and drive off.

The screaming and moaning continue from upstairs. It is Georgie. Margaret knows it is Georgie. What is that woman doing to him? she thinks frantically. Whatever it is, it can't be good. Steeling herself, Margaret rings the doorbell. The moaning cuts off mid-gasp. Margaret hears the slamming of a door and a gentle thumping from inside the house. The front door swings open.

It's Claudia.

The woman's hair floats around her head like fiery-orange snakes. Her eyes are shadowed with purple circles, her freckles strain to jump off of her parchment-white skin.

"Uh, hi ". . .," Margaret begins.

"What do you want?" Claudia interrupts.

Margaret stares open-mouthed at the woman. "Georgie," she finally sputters. She stands up a little straighter. "I wanted to talk to Georgie?"

"He's not home," Claudia says impatiently. Her eyes narrow, her message clear. *Scram.*

"But I heard him," Margaret insists, almost choking on the words. Claudia's eyes are like smoldering coals. Margaret cringes back from them but refuses to leave.

"Did you?" Claudia raises an eyebrow. Then she sighs. Her face softens into a small smile. "I suppose you did."

Margaret can't help but relax slightly at Claudia's sudden change of attitude, although she is still terrified of the woman.

"Why don't you sit down?" Claudia gestures gently to one of the porch chairs. Margaret collapses into it weakly; Claudia's smile increases slightly. To Margaret, the woman's canines seem pointed, wolf-like.

"Georgie has not been feeling very well lately," Claudia explains.

Margaret raises her eyebrows and opens her mouth to express her worry, but Claudia cuts her off.

"Not that. Mentally, he is fine. It's just, uh, the flu. A really bad case of the flu. That's what the noise is from. It's hurting him a lot."

Margaret gasps. "Shouldn't he be in the hospital, if it's that bad?"

Claudia shakes her head. "I took him there last night. But you know Georgie—he can't stand the hospital." She smiles. "They sent me home with instructions for caring for him, and I know who to call if he takes a turn for the worst. But they say he should pull through all right. It just has to hurt him a bit, first, before he can get better."

"Can I see him?" Margaret says.

"No," Claudia says, her breathing becomes short, and her eyes go wild for a moment. "He's really contagious." Claudia's eyes narrow evilly. "Trust me; you don't want to catch this one."

Margaret nods slowly; then her own eyes narrow with suspicion. "I just saw Georgie yesterday, at the grocery store," she says. "He seemed fine."

Claudia seems shocked for a moment. And then . . . Is that jealousy? Is she actually jealous of Margaret?

(I don't know, Ben. Is it? Does Claudia love Georgie, really?

Who can really love Georgie, doc? He isn't real. Remember? Who can love what isn't even there?

And what does love have to do with jealousy anyway?)

Margaret starts. What can Claudia have to be jealous of?

"It came on quickly," Claudia says, her smile stiffening, her sharp teeth glistening. Margaret shudders. "In the afternoon. I took him to the hospital last night; they sent him home this morning."

Margaret nods again. What else can she do? Claudia's story is airtight.

"Will you tell him I came by to see him?" Margaret says. "Tell him that I'm worried about him and I hope he gets better soon."

Claudia's grin widens triumphantly. "Oh, I will. I'm sure that he'll be back on his feet in no time." Claudia rises from her chair.

Margaret stands with her but doesn't move away. She hesitates a moment, looking up to the bedroom window, wondering.

Georgie has been absolutely silent since Claudia came to the door. Almost as if . . .

"Goodbye," Claudia says pointedly, showing her teeth.

(Parenthetical Pet Peeve) People who say "Bub Bye."

"Yes." Margaret jumps a little, and takes a few steps back. "Yes, goodbye."

. . . as if Claudia is the one who is causing his pain.

Margaret puts as much feeling as she can into her next words. "I'm sure we'll see each other again soon," she says.

Claudia's face seems to indicate that she would rather not, but Margaret doesn't see; she is already halfway down the sidewalk, running for the street.

When she hears the front door slam, Margaret sneaks back up to the side of the house. After a moment, she hears Georgie begin to moan again. He actually screams. The sound reminds her of a terrified child.

With this proof in her pocket, Margaret flees the sounds of her friend's pain.

That night, Georgie dozes on his bed. He feels his cuts oozing slowly into the bandages Claudia applied so expertly. The tingling, burning pain consumes his whole mind. He relaxes into the sensation, wrapping it around him like a blanket. A fuzzy, pinching, biting blanket.

The doorbell rings. Georgie dimly hears Claudia's voice as she answers.

A loud, booming male voice answers hers. Georgie perks up a little. He wonders if it is an old boyfriend. Claudia answers the voice, but it insists. The door opens, and two sets of loud footsteps clomp on the hardwood floors.

A soft knock on the door, and Claudia pokes her head in.

"I'm so sorry, dear, but there are some officers here to see you," she says, in the kindest, most gentle voice that Georgie has ever heard her use.

"What?" he says groggily.

"He's sick," she explains to someone behind her. "You can't just come in. You might catch it."

"We'll take our chances, Ma'am," the booming voice says.

Georgie sighs. "They can come in, Claudia," he says.

Two blue-suits tromp into the room in heavy black shoes. When they see Georgie lying on the bed, they exchange glances.

"We're sorry to bother you, sir," says the first suit. His voice is quiet, but serious. "I am Detective Marley, and this is my partner, Officer Carver."

Detective Marley is thin, with a mustache. Georgie wants to laugh at him, but remembers to play his part.

"Is everything okay? What's wrong?" he says weakly.

"There's been a report of domestic violence," Carver begins, his voice filling up the room. He is a large man, with a shock of black hair that sticks straight up towards the ceiling.

"What? Claudia?" Georgie looks over at her.

"It wasn't me, darling," she says innocently.

He wonders if this is a new sort of torture. Maybe she will send him to jail, and let the inmates and the guards do the torturing for her. He would have to pay her double for that, maybe even an extra grand as congratulations for her genius. She's riding me all the way to the bank, he thinks lazily. Then Georgie realizes that the cops are staring at him.

"I never hit her," he stammers. "Not once."

The officers glance at one another. Detective Marley turns around.

"Would you mind leaving us, Ms Nesbitt?" he says calmly.

Claudia looks at Georgie. He shrugs weakly.

"Don't be too hard on him," Claudia says. "He's in very fragile condition."

She walks over to Georgie's side and kisses his forehead, just like she loves him, just like she cares for him. So this is what it would be like, Georgie thinks wonderingly, amazed at the momentary bliss that floods him at her gentle touch. Then she leaves, closing the door quietly behind her. When the latch clicks closed, both cops direct their attention entirely to Georgie.

"The tip wasn't about you abusing Claudia," Marley says. "It was about her abusing you."

For a moment, Georgie can't even speak. He stares at them both. A hysterical chuckle rises in his throat, but he disguises it as a cough.

"That's ridiculous," he says finally.

Marley shrugs. "Maybe."

Carver pulls out a pad of paper from his breast pocket. "Just what is your relationship with Ms Nesbitt?" he asks, his pen poised above the paper.

"She's my girlfriend. She lives here with me," Georgie says. She's my tormentor, my torturer, he wants to say. She's my love and hate, my twisted perverted sex goddess. Don't judge her, officers. I asked her to.

(Do you think there are people judging you, Ben?

Of course there are, Dr C. Aren't you judging me? Isn't that what this is all about?)

Carver scratches down his answer on the pad.

"Does she ever hit you, Mr Gust?" Carver continues.

"Of course not," Georgie says. This time, he really does laugh, although he's not sure why. "Look at her! Sh-she couldn't hurt a spider."

The cops take a moment to think as one of their radios buzzes an encrypted message.

"There are many different ways of hurting the ones we love," Marley says quietly, with an understanding smile.

"Love?" Georgie says quietly, pretending to mull it over. "Yeah. Love . . . ."

Marley and Carver shake their heads. Clearly, the man is a goner.

"Do you have any reason to believe that Ms Nesbitt would want to hurt you, Mr Gust?" Carver asks brusquely.

"Oh really, is this necessary?" Georgie says in a brash tone. He hopes his façade is intact.

Marley smiles again, seeming to agree with Georgie at the ridiculousness of the questioning.

"It's just part of the routine," he says. "Paperwork, you know."

"Shouldn't you see a doctor?" Carver interrupts. "You look pretty sick."

Georgie readjusts the bunched-up pillow under his elbow and shrugs. "I-I feel better today than yesterday. I'll be f-fine."

The officers exchange a look when they hear his stutter.

"Sir, I think you should see a doctor," Marley says. "You don't look too great to me."

"What do you shiteheads know about it?" Georgie cries out. Then he closes his eyes.

Marley whispers something to Carver. Georgie can't hear most of it, but the word "poison" passes his lips.

He laughs. "You two are really something. Really," he says. "You're not going to get me into the hospital. I'm fine. Everything's fine here. My girlfriend is not beating me, or torturing me, or even making me mad. Most of the time."

He laughs loudly at his own joke, but Carver and Marley will not laugh with him.

He sobers up. "In any case, you two are completely out of line here. I have no intention of charging my girlfriend with abuse, nor do I have any reason to. Now if you'd please . . ."

The officers look at each other in confusion.

" . . . get out," Georgie finishes.

They stand, but hesitate.

"Get out!" he screams.

Claudia opens the door with a bang. "What are you doing to him in here?" she demands.

"Out!" Georgie screams again.

His screams and her nagging tone follow the officers all the way out the door and to the street.

Dr C Goes Deep

"Ben," Dr C says finally, one day. For a long time she just listened as I told the story, but today . . .

"Ben," she says.

"Yeah?"

"Ben," she draws the word out, spends a long time saying my name. "Ben," she repeats, "why is the driver named Ben?"

I look at her. She is going nuts again.

"Why is anyone named anything?" I point out. "Why was I named Ben?"

She pushes her lips together.

"Is there a story there, behind your name?" she asks.

Dr C is some kind of detective, but she is always digging in the wrong direction, if you ask me.

(Parenthetical Pet Peeve) When naming a child, people who give no thought as to how name will sound with their surname. For example: Dick Hertz, Mike Hunt, etc.

"Family name," I explain. "We're all a bunch of inbred blue bloods, you know. Too many names would be tough to remember."

Her lip quivers a bit. One of these days, I will get her to smile.

"Why is the driver named Ben?" she repeats. "Is it a family name for him, too?"

"How the heck should I know?" I retort. "You don't see me or Georgie talking much to Ben, do you?"

"Maybe that's the problem," she muses.

"What?"

I swear, the woman has really lost her mind this time.

"Ben, are you Georgie's driver?"

I laugh. "Uh, no, Dr C. I haven't been driving since the robbery. You know that."

She waves me off. "No, Ben. What I'm asking, are you the vehicle, and Georgie rides around in you. That is why Ben's the driver, right?"

"I don't know, Dr C."

It is a hell of a lot more complicated than that.

Dear Diary:

Cool? Fuck cool. I'm awesome.

Love Can Keep Them Together

In her dream, Claudia is having dinner with the Gusts. Only instead of the ham or roasted pig on the table, this time it's Georgie who's curled up on a large serving platter, an apple shoved between his teeth.

(Parenthetical Pet Peeve) "Delicious" apples. They aren't.

His skin is still crackling, roasted to perfection. His eyes are glassy, sightless. Georgie's mother approaches with a carving knife and fork, crisscrossing their edges, sharpening one against the other. She poises over Georgie.

"I'm so glad you're not one of those vegetarians," she says, grinning horribly. "I just wanted to thank ya for taking such good care of our Geow-gie," she says and then slices downward with a flash of steel.

Georgie squeals his pain and Claudia jerks out of bed. She glances at the lump that is Georgie, his screeching still echoing between her ears.

"I am sorry," she whispers. "I am so sorry . . . ."

With a glass of wine in her hand, Claudia mopes around Georgie's bungalow. It's nothing like what she had expected.

The sterile counters are not clean because someone cares for the place and its inhabitants, someone who tenderly scrubs down the surfaces with loving consideration. No. The counters are clean because no one uses them, because the place is devoid of life. No one actually lives there.

Claudia and Georgie drift around the place like ghosts, replaying the tortures of ages past. Claudia wonders if Georgie still feels the pain, if he still gets off to it. As for her, she doesn't feel the satisfaction of torturing him anymore. Georgie is no longer every man who has hurt her, and hurting him is no longer a way to get back at every evil she has ever known. Georgie is just the man who's tangled up in her life right now, the man she can't seem to convince herself to leave. Like all the others. She loves him.

Still. She's being paid to torture him, so that's what she'll do.

Walking into the cluttered yet organized living room, Claudia kicks over a stack of Georgie's sketches. Let that be the latest blow, she thinks to herself. Now he'll have to stack it all back up. She snickers to herself. Any petty meanness can be justified, but that doesn't make it right. Claudia drains her glass of wine as she hears Georgie's alarm go off. The digital clock on the wall reads: 10:00 am. She thinks about starting a pot of coffee but, still frustrated, she opts for more booze and considers how she might torture Georgie this evening.

"Screw pain," she thinks. She is not into pain, not tonight.

That night, when Georgie walks in expecting dinner, Claudia breezes past him on her way out the door.

"Where you going?" Georgie says, confusion all over his face.

"None of your business," Claudia grins wolfishly. "Don't I get a night off every now and then?"

He can smell that she has been drinking, but then so has he. She is wearing tight jeans that show her pudgy bottom, her thick thighs. A scanty halter shows the small roll of fat at the back of her shoulders. Georgie wants to laugh at her, a little. But he thinks that maybe—just maybe—some other man might find her attractive. If he had been drinking; if she was just his type.

(I thought she was your type, Georgie? Older, unfettered . . . nice feet?)

Georgie tells that voice in his head to shut it. You live with a woman long enough, and her skin doesn't seem all that sexy anymore. In fact, it can just about make you puke.

"Sure," he grins, diabolically. "I could use a night off, too."

He flashes her a lopsided grin as she leaves, imagining her being unsettled by his cavalier attitude, then decides it's more likely that she doesn't give a shite one way or the other. Probably, she just needs a break, like she said. Maybe.

Claudia slides into the greasy, sleazy bar like she owns the place. It's been months since old Claudia has been around. For a minute everyone looks up, surprised to see her. Within seconds, the novelty of Claudia's reappearance is gone, and the crowd goes back to what they all do best—drink. Claudia fits right in; her favorite stool still bears her name.

"Gin gimlet," she orders, her green eyes glistening.

The bartender, although drunk, is not quite as gone as the other regulars. He looks at her, tilting his head slightly.

"Been a while," he says gruffly, pouring her drink.

"Yeah, guess so." She grins at him. Damn it feels good to be out again. On the prowl, Claudia thinks. Rawr.

She shifts her shoulders easily, feeling the stale bar air on her exposed skin. She can feel eyes on her, but she's not here for just any old fling.

Oh no. Claudia has a particular gentleman in mind for tonight. She has a plan, and she is sticking to it.

Of course, she started the night early in order to work up her resolve, in order to keep Georgie from sucking her into his company. After a few drinks, she plays a round or two of darts, a little pool, then bangs around the jukebox for a minute or two, catching up with the regulars. There is nothing new in their lives, luckily, nothing to catch up on except the same old shite played over and over again. And, luckily for Claudia, they are all so wasted that they can't remember what she has told them, so she tells them everything and more than everything. She tells them everything she wishes she had the nerve to do to Georgie, but can't. Then a few minutes later, one of them will stagger over to her again and say: "Hey, Claudia, how the hell you been?" and she can start it all over again.

Maybe talking about it is better than living it; she wonders if Georgie would modify the deal to make imagining new tortures, without actually doing them, a still-payable offense.

She knows the answer to that before she even begins.

Claudia sighs and puts her chin in her hands. With her elbows on the bar, she sips deeply from her fourth gin gimlet. She is starting to warm up to it. Her shoulders slouch. Her belt pulls in at her gut, cutting off circulation to her nether regions.

The door creaks open, and in walk her lucky pair.

Claudia smiles to see their faces, their arms wrapped around each other. They're so damn happy, she thinks. She knows she wouldn't hate them nearly as much if they weren't so damn happy all the time. She glowers a little, until they notice her. She arranges her face.

"Greg! Sara!" she calls. "Over here, you two!"

With intoxicated smiles, Greg and Sara float over to where Claudia waits. Maybe they are dumb, or maybe they're too trusting, or maybe Claudia never got a chance to tell them everything she thought of them. They don't seem to think that there is anything wrong with the picture of Claudia waving to them and hollering friendly greetings at the top of her lungs.

"Claudia," Sara gushes.

"Claudia," Greg belches. "How the hell have you been? We haven't seen you in ages."

"Yeah," Claudia says. "I guess because I got fired."

Sara and Greg look at her for a moment with fixed terror. Then Claudia laughs, and they both laugh with her. They are captivated by her, her wild hair, her free spirit. Her open toes beckon to them both.

"Claudia, I'm so sorry," Greg says presently. "I don't know what I was thinking, back then. It was such a terrible mistake."

Claudia grins easily. It is not Greg that she loves and hates; it is not Greg that she wants to make suffer anymore. It is Georgie—just Georgie. And for now, that means that Greg is forgiven. Sara, too. By default. Claudia puts a hand on each of their legs and leans into them, breathing her hot, ginny breath in their direction.

"That's all in the past," she insists, her vocal cords humming. Greg and Sara croon along with her.

"Oh, I'm so glad," Sara says. Her eyes shine bright. "I've missed our friendship."

Claudia wants to laugh at the woman who can call their love and hate relationship a friendship. *(Maybe you can, though. Maybe you should.)* But instead, she just smiles and keeps her features smooth. "This round's on me," she says.

The three former lovers sidle up to the bar, whispering and pointing fingers and bursting into loud laughter.

"And then my house burned down," Claudia yells finally. Greg and Sara crack up. "Can you believe it?" she goads them.

Wordlessly, with tears streaming from their eyes, they shake their heads.

"Claudia, you live such a crazy life," Sara says, giggling.

"Yeah well, it gets better," Claudia grins. "Now I'm living with the guy who burned my house down."

"Oh, you're not," Sara insists.

Greg laughs out loud. "Of course she is."

"You should come stay with us," Sara squeals. In her drunken haze, she thinks this is a good idea.

Claudia waves the woman down. "Oh, I am feeling really settled where I am. Georgie—that's his name—he's actually such a sweet man. Like an uncle, really."

Her eyes light up, almost as if she had come up with an idea on the spot. "Hey, you guys should meet him," she says. "How about tonight?"

Greg and Sara nod enthusiastically.

"I have got to meet this guy," Greg says.

"All right." Claudia smiles. "One more shot and then we're out of here."

Greg and Sara nod again, their eyelids drooping. Half an hour later, the three stagger in the dark towards the front door of Georgie's house. One of the shadowed figures giggles then stumbles into a bush.

"Sara!" One of the other shadows laughs helplessly then bends down to scoop her up.

Claudia's shadow strides purposefully up the front steps, tripping only slightly on her way. Georgie sits in his dark office with his feet on the desktop that shimmers from the light of three video cameras—cameras that he now addresses, cameras that have been set up (that have always been set up) for the single purpose of recording him and perhaps, perhaps, catching a moment of sanity.

You never know—it could work.

But at the moment, Georgie is as schizo as ever, babbling on into the night about what a poor, tortured creature he is under Claudia, how even her leaving him for a night is still a torment to him. Poor, poor Georgie. And then he hears the voices at the front door.

When he recognizes Claudia's voice among them, Georgie relaxes. But only slightly. Regardless of what he has been saying to the cameras, about how being apart from Claudia is torture in itself, he really doesn't want to face her, now or ever. He can't imagine what new torture she has cooked up for him, and he doesn't want to learn.

Georgie dives under his desk when he hears the footsteps climbing the stairs to the second floor. Just as he manages to tuck his feet in behind him, exposing his pudgy bottom to the coldness of the hard wood floor, the door slams open.

"Georgie," Claudia calls drunkenly. There is giggling behind her. "Georgie Porgie." She snorts with laughter. "Huh, where is that little muffin? My uncle-type, that is. My funny uncle."

Another explosion of laughter from the hallway, and Claudia exits, leaving the door partially open. Georgie squeezes his eyelids tight shut. He hardly dares to breathe until he hears their voices in the next room.

Then he stands and crawls to the cameras. He stands up next to the one on the left, which is positioned in such a way that he can jump behind the door if anyone comes.

"You see what I'm talking about?" he whispers into the camera. Hearing noises coming from Claudia's room, he detaches the camera from its tripod and creeps down the hallway.

"I'll sh-show you," Georgie whispers. His heart hammers in his chest.

When he gets to the doorway, he can hear Claudia moaning. He knows what is going on but can't stop himself from opening the door, anyway. It's one aspect of the part he plays, the part they play together.

The room is dark, but the moonlight glows through the single window. Claudia and her two lovers are entwined, like one massive, gyrating, screeching creature. Georgie trains the camera steadily on the beast.

"You bitch," he screeches, hardly recognizing his own voice.

The beast barely acknowledges him; it just keeps right on.

"You bitch!"

Georgie is screaming, although there is no sound . . . .

When Claudia wakes up the next morning, her unexpected doubled pay awaits her on her bedside table. Georgie is nowhere to be seen. Claudia thumbs through the cash. If the insurance doesn't come through on the house in another year or so, she will still have enough money to build a new one at this rate.

If she can make it that long. If she can stick to sleeping around and skip the cigarette burns and the S&M shite, she decides she can make it. After all, sleeping around's not that hard.

Georgie can't even look at Claudia, let alone talk to her about what happened.

He mopes up and down the aisles at the grocery store, but Margaret is nowhere to be seen. It's not her shopping day.

Georgie considers waiting around until she does show up. It will only be a day, maybe two days. The store is open 24 hours a day. Georgie could live off the free samples and produce and fresh-baked bread until Margaret shows up. Margaret will know what to do, Georgie thinks. Margaret will fuck me; she'll make Claudia look like a two-bit hooker, an over-the-hill beauty queen. Georgie knows that Margaret will never fuck him, not in a million years. But she might give him some relief, just a little relief.

Then Georgie, still moping up and down the aisles, realizes that Claudia might end up at the store, too. He has never seen her there before, but you never know. It's something new with Claudia every day, and maybe first thing on today's list is to go shopping. Georgie rockets out of the grocery store like a cat out of a bathtub.

Where does Georgie go to avoid Claudia?

To the same places he used to go. Georgie slides into place in his old haunts, the sicko-twisted sex clubs of his past, like a foot sliding into an old shoe. He walks up to his favorite, a century-old wooden house with a maze of rooms on the top floor. He sighs as his foot hits the third step—a rotted, warped piece of wood that creaks every time his foot hits it. It's as though nothing has changed.

The club is not a business on the outside, but a private residence. Nothing to see here, ma'am—just us lonely, heartbroken suckers for pain, having a friendly get-together.

"Hello, Mr Gust," says the woman who sits at the foot of the stairs. "We haven't seen you here for quite some time."

"I've been busy," Georgie says, grinning at the woman.

In these places, Georgie doesn't feel quite like the self that he presents to the rest of the world. In this house, filled with sicko-twisted perverts with their nauseating fantasies, Georgie feels quite suave. Almost normal.

"Is Samantha here?" he asks, in the mood for a good old-fashioned foot smothering.

"Hm, Samantha has a prior engagement," the woman says, consulting her clipboard. "How about Alia?"

Georgie shrugs. "Whatever," he says.

The woman shows him to a private room—a small room, with a queen-sized bed, large closet, and several mirrors.

"Alia will be in shortly," the woman says. With an artificial smile, she leaves.

Georgie sits on the bed and waits. After a few minutes, he lies on his back and stares up at the mirrored ceiling, which stares back impassively.

Georgie looks up at his own face. It's not a bad face, he thinks, although he has a hard time believing that it's really his.

Finally, the door opens again.

"Alia?" Georgie asks. He props himself up on his elbows.

"That's me," the girl says.

She is dark-skinned and petite, with bleached blonde hair or a wig—Georgie can't decide which.

"Huh," Georgie says.

Alia walks closer to him. "You wanted a foot smothering?"

"Yes . . . well, no." Georgie's thoughts are racing. "I changed my mind. Is that okay?"

Alia smiles softly. "Well, that depends on what you want me to do," she says.

"Tie me up. Cut me. Burn me. Whip me," Georgie entreats her. He can't meet her gaze. Instead, he glances over at the bedside table. Propped on it is another mirror, a small round hand mirror. Georgie's face surprises him again.

"Oh, you want it rough today, is that it?" Alia purrs. "Well, I think I can manage that, Mr Gust. Yes, indeed . . . ."

Georgie watches with detachment as Alia ties his hands with handkerchiefs to the bedposts, avoiding her eyes and his own, which, if he could stand to look in the mirror again, would beg him to stop. To come to his senses.

Claudia brought this on herself, he reminds himself. She cheated first, with those . . . those . . .

Georgie remembers the sight of the beast and anger flares hot in him. He clenches his fist and rattles the bedpost.

"Hm, someone's getting excited," Alia notes. She slowly undoes the buttons of Georgie's shirt. Then she pulls a penknife from the top drawer of the bedside table. She draws the blade gently across his chest. It is just a tickle, just a reminder of what pain could really be.

She is too soft, too gentle, this Alia. She lacks Claudia's rough edge, her true penchant for pain. She probably never gets angry, this girl . . . just uses her soft voice, the voice of reason, to keep everyone under control.

"Do you do hypnotism?" Georgie blurts out.

Alia lays a hand on his shoulder and smiles. "Afraid not."

She draws the knife a little harder now, causing a bit of a burn on his skin. She uses the sharp tip to prick at his collarbone. Georgie feels a small bit of wetness where she has been; he groans with the release that this gives him. Claudia will flow out of him as his blood leaks through fresh cuts. Maybe he will forget all about Claudia. Maybe Alia will do the trick.

"You like that, huh?" she encourages him. She scratches his neck and throat with her fingernails. "Yeah, you do."

Then she stops for a moment. She dips her fingernail into one of the small drops of blood oozing from Georgie's chest, where she pricked him. She draws a tiny, thin line across his throat.

"What is your safe word?" she asks finally.

"What?" Georgie says wonderingly. "Safe word?"

How could anything in this world be made safe?

"You know," Alia explains. "The word you say to make me stop? If things get too rough for you?"

"What?" Georgie understands now, but he is too incensed to respond properly. "Untie me," he commands her.

Biting her lip, Alia slowly complies. Georgie sits up abruptly once he is free, buttoning his shirt with rapid hands.

"I think that's enough for today," he says in a huff, as he stands.

"I'm sorry, was it something I did?" Alia asks. "Don't go. I'll do it right next time. Just tell me what I did."

Georgie turns in the doorway. "A safe word?" He scoffs at the thought. "You've got to be kidding me."

After his encounter with Alia, Georgie gets down and dirty. Only the worst of the worst will do it for him. He could not stand to sit and be "tortured" by another nice girl. He sits through innumerable foot smotherings. He is tied down, cut up, forced to crawl across hard rock crystals—all before the anonymity of strangers.

The strangers are a nice touch, Georgie thinks. They add an element of humiliation to the situation that a private room never could.

But Georgie is even less fulfilled now than he was before he met Claudia. Before Claudia, Georgie did not know what good was. Now he watches all his so-called tormentors, his fellow sufferers, and he feels nothing but contempt. These masochists do not know what it is like to have a Claudia on their chest, digging holes into their hearts. They do not know what it is like to have her in their oxygen, destroying their perfectly controlled environments. They have not woken up locked in a closet or naked in the street. They are vacationing masochists, dabbling in a pastime they do not even understand. They don't know what pain is; they don't have the slightest clue.

They are weak. Georgie has outgrown them.

By the end of the week, Georgie has had enough of the same old S&M fetish houses. He wants the big guns, something he has never seen before-something that is bound to shake him up.

He takes the recommendation of a friend (if you could call him a friend), who gives him a phone number without a name.

"Just trust me," the guy says, shaking visibly. "This is some heavy shite, here. If this doesn't shake you up, then you must be dead."

Georgie finds hope in this promise. He calls the number and is sent straight to voicemail—a lonely mechanized voice repeats the dialed number to him, then commands him to leave a message. There is the beep.

"Hey, uh . . . my name is Georgie Gust. I-I got your number from a friend of mine. Looking for something to shake me up. Looking for some heavy shite, you know. He told me you could help ". . . ." Georgie trails off. Without a name, without even knowing what the number can offer him, he doesn't have a clue.

"Can you?" he concludes lamely. "Can you? Help me, I mean. Th-thank-thank you."

An hour later, Georgie gets a text message with an address, a date, and a time.

Georgie's shiny black limo winds its way through a forest of pine trees. Up, up they climb until the trees dwindle into small, gnarled grey things, and rocks begin to jut up from the lichened earth.

The road grows increasingly narrow, the cement finally dissolving into a single-lane gravel road. The road rises high above the rocky ground then meets the towering metal doorway of a thick granite wall.

Ben gets out and presses the buzzer beside the doorway then gets back in the limousine and drives it backwards about 10 feet. The metal doorway slowly opens outward, revealing a circular plot of land surrounded by the wall.

Ben creeps forward, following the narrow dirt road that hugs the interior of the wall. In the center of the circle sits a sizeable stone cottage. Ben completes the circle while Georgie stares out the driver's side window, studying the cottage from every angle. Soon, Ben has the limo turned around and is facing the road once more, ready to drift back down the mountain. He opens the door for Georgie, who crawls out slowly and unsteadily.

Georgie strolls to the front door of the cottage. It is made of thick, dark wood and has a heavy, round, brass knocker in the center. Georgie stares at the knocker for a moment then lifts it. With a blink, he drops the knocker. It thuds hollowly when it strikes. Georgie waits, shivering a little at the coldness of the rock walls. It is not long before the door creaks open, revealing a haggard woman of indeterminable age, bent at the waist in an effort to open the door. Georgie is amazed that she is capable of pulling the huge thing open at all.

"I'm G-Georgie. Georgie Gust," he says. "I'm here to, uh . . ."

"I know what you're here for," the woman says with a toothless grin. "Come in. It will only be a minute."

She gestures to a sagging chair in the corner and shuffles off to the back.

Georgie sits in the chair with a loud thump, sending a cloud of dust into the air. Georgie coughs, starts to chokes, as the particles clog his lungs.

(Parenthetical Pet Peeve) Going to work and realizing I forgot to use deodorant.

When the dust settles, Georgie looks around in alarm. The walls are dirty, covered in soot; bits of paper and clumps of dirt and pine needles are scattered across the tabletops and floor. The whole place smells like something inside the walls has died, or maybe it's the bearskin rug in front of the fireplace. Georgie wonders if the rug has ever been properly cleaned; he imagines bits of fat and meat still clinging to the underside of the fur. Bile rises in his throat as he thinks of it, and yet Georgie finds himself strangely turned on by the filth. It is strange and new—a different kind of pain, the fear of the filth that now surrounds him. He rejoices in the newness of the feeling. His penis swells.

The woman returns. She is naked, but covered in a shining film that might be—Georgie's nose twitches—lube. The woman has drowned herself in shining, slippery lubricant; it glistens from the caverns of her wrinkled skin, drips from her sagging breasts, which swing pendulum-like. Georgie can't help but stare at them, fixated. They hypnotize him. Georgie wonders if their swinging can reverse the naked sleepwalking thing that Claudia's trained his subconscious to employ.

The woman is as filthy as the cabin, if not more so. Grime clots her wrinkles and lint is trapped by the lube across her vast belly. Her forward-jutting chest tapers to a sagging, concave backside, with flesh that seems to drip from her bones like seaweed. As she reaches for Georgie, the dirt beneath her fingernails seems to grow, to stretch, reaching for him. Georgie can't move; he stands staring, transfixed, couldn't look away if his life depended on it. The woman rips the clothes from his body, tearing the buttons off his shirt, and breaking a nail—dirt still embedded beneath it—on his belt buckle.

"Whoops-a-daisy," she cackles, then whips off his belt.

Georgie is a statue, frozen. His cock stands erect in the cold mountain air. He has prepared himself for anything to happen in this place, and the fact that this old woman presents herself as lust-worthy doesn't faze him. Nothing can, not after Claudia.

Georgie can tell this old woman used to be trouble; she was a pair of double Ds who could get anything she wanted with a wink and a giggle. But time and gravity have betrayed her, have dragged her sideways and down; until now she looks more animal than human. And now—now that men no longer want her, will no longer have her, she'll have them.

Georgie is locked in her gaze. Snakelike, she slithers before him. Her arms wrap around and around him, pulling him tight to her, choking off his air. He is drawn into her flesh—the lubricated rolls and wrinkles mold around him. He can't breathe—he doesn't need to. She will breathe for both of them.

With nothing but a smile she heaves him to the rug and then swallows him whole.

Dear Diary:

Sometimes I wish I had a mother. I never knew her. Since I was a little boy. I wish I had someone who made the choice every day to put my happiness and well-being ahead of their own, to teach me the hard lessons, and to do the right thing even when he or she is not sure what the right thing is . . . . And to forgive me—and his or her self over and over again for everything wrong.

Nothing But a Brilliant, Bright Prick of Light

The rancid scent of an unwashed creature brings Georgie to his senses; he is nose-deep in the bearskin rug. Groaning, he pushes himself to his knees. He is naked, covered in lube and lint, bear fur, and dust. He vomits into the bear fur, realizes what the smell truly is, and vomits again.

The woman lies before him on the rug, illuminated by the rays of morning sunshine that dance mockingly through the grimy window. She quivers a moment, mumbles incoherently. Her hand twitches, her fingers crawl across the rug to find him. Slowly she reaches for the pile of vomit that Georgie's left (his is not the first one, of course. That is what the smell is). With a stifled yelp, Georgie leaps to his feet and runs to the front door.

The woman's hand finds the pile of vomit. "Fer chrissakes," she moans. "What the fuck is that?"

Georgie presses frantically at the door handle, shoving into the heavy wooden door with his shoulder.

"Hey, yore not leaving' so soon, are ya?" she looks up and grins. Her gaping mouth is a cavernous black hole. She will swallow him again.

With a cry and renewed vigor, Georgie shoves at the door. It won't budge. She is standing now. She is coming after him. Georgie wishes that he lifted weights, that he had the almighty strength to push open this door with a single stroke of his arm. The woman, the hag, the creature is almost upon him, her fingers, still vomit-covered, reach for him.

Georgie screams like a trapped animal. He pushes against the door again and again. It won't open. It won't open. And then . . . Then he remembers, he has to pull. He has to pull the door open. Success. The door opens easily. Light slashes through and the woman shrieks, raising a hand to her eyes as Georgie races to his limo and safety.

Ben looks up groggily as Georgie slams his palm against the door. Ben seems to be laughing at him, laughing as he unlocks the back door. The woman—whom Georgie has begun to think of as 'the creature'—appears in the doorway to the cottage, and Ben raises an eyebrow.

Ben's attitude is wasted on Georgie, who yanks the door open and collapses inside the limo with a gasp and a long, whimpering sigh.

"G-get the h-hell out of here," he commands. When Ben locks the doors and begins to roll out of the driveway, Georgie sinks into the seat. His arms and legs are buzzing, weak from exertion. He slips into blackness, into nothingness, eternity.

[Smoke Break]

When Georgie comes to, Ben is pulling in front of his house; it is noon, the sun overhead glares down, making the world too bright, too harsh. With a groan, Georgie pulls himself out of the car. Ben helps him walk inside. Claudia is not there, leaving him feeling relieved yet sad as well.

Considering what he has been through, a little reassurance would do him some good, but Claudia is not there, and neither is Margaret. The only reassurance Georgie has is himself, and he is no consolation at all. Not to anyone. Georgie crawls upstairs and into bed and falls asleep immediately.

Ben pauses for a moment in the doorway.

"Poor son of a bitch," he mutters.

When Georgie wakes again, it is nearly 5:00 am; the sun is setting, and its light gleams orange through his blinds. He rolls over, trying to convince himself that the cottage, the woman—the creature—were not real, that the whole thing was just a dream. But when he looks down at himself, at his still-slick skin, and smells the stench of bear fur and vomit, he knows that it happened.

This makes him want to break down and sob his heart out, but he can't. He can't even bring himself to cry. Eventually he gets out of bed and staggers into the bathroom. He turns the water to hot, sits on the toilet, and waits for the shower to steam then climbs in.

Claudia is still not home. Georgie putters around his house, stacking up his physics notes into neat, uncluttered piles, putting Claudia's books back in their rightful places on the bookshelves. He thinks about going back to bed, even stands in the bedroom door, staring at the rumpled mess of his blankets. But the stench of himself, of the woman—the creature—is in the sheets, so he rips them from the bed and stuffs them in the hamper and remakes the bed. Still, the stink of the old woman's cottage clings to him. Georgie grabs the new sheets off the bed, turning his nose away from the smell. Claudia is still not home, and no matter where he goes, the smell clings to him.

These sheets, Georgie tosses into an old metal barrel he keeps stored in his shed. He dumps a canister of lighter fluid on the sheets then lights a cigarette. The smoke fills his lungs and his soul. Georgie begins to calm; the shaking in his fingers ceases. Halfway through the cigarette, Georgie grins sadly and tosses the last of the burning cigarette into the barrel. He jumps backwards as the pile of sheets explodes in a ball of flames. It's like a huge candle, Georgie thinks to himself, the biggest candle this backyard has ever seen.

Georgie lights a second cigarette, and sits on his back step to watch the fire die. Claudia comes home during Georgie's second shower. He hears the front door open and close. Please, God, he pleads. Just let her go easy on me today. He can hear as Claudia hollers his name. I'll do anything just make her go easy on me. I'll go to church . . . anything. The sound of her clomping footsteps on the stairs makes his heart skip.

I'll even pray. C'mon . . . we got a deal?

There is no answer, but . . .

"Georgie," Claudia says softly. Her voice sounds like an angel's.

Georgie peeks through the glass shower door. Through the hazy shower steam, Claudia's face glows. Her eyes are wide and luminous, a child's eyes.

"Georgie, I know you're in there," she teases. "Can I come in, too?"

"Uh, sure," he croaks. He cracks the door open an inch.

"Georgie, I missed you," Claudia purrs as she steps inside.

She is still fully clothed. Immediately, her clothes gets drenched with the hot water.

"Did you?" Georgie's voice sounds strange even to his own ears. "Where were you?"

"Ah, now. That's a secret," Claudia says, putting a finger to his lips. Slowly, she pulls her wet sweater over her head. She is wearing a white cotton bra, and her nipples poke out through the wet cloth.

Pencil erasers, Georgie thinks.

"After all, it's not like you're going to tell me where you have been?" Claudia continues.

Georgie stares at her for a minute. She gives him a secret little smile. She already knows. Maybe Ben told her. Georgie sighs.

"No," he says.

"Well, what makes you think that where I've been has been anything better?" Claudia whispers. "Maybe I really missed you, you know. Maybe I'm tired of all this. Maybe I'm just looking for a break, for a bit of relief. It's tiring keeping you happy all the time, Mr Georgie."

She laughs, but he can hardly blame her.

"I'm a little tired, myself," Georgie admits. He sets his hands on her waist. With a groan, he buries his head in her breasts, fumbling with the clasps at the back of her bra. She replaces his hands with her own nimble fingers; he sinks to his knees, clutching at her, resting his head against her soft belly.

"Claudia," he mutters softly.

Suddenly she has stepped out of her jeans—how he doesn't know. She lifts him up with her gentle hands; he finds himself hardening under her fingertips.

"How about some good old-fashioned lovemaking?" Claudia whispers, nibbling at his ear. "I think that's just the ticket."

Georgie groans and nods. He presses against her.

"The condoms," he mutters. He reaches for the shower door.

"Not so fast, Georgie Porgie!" Claudia insists. She holds the door handle firmly in place. How'd she get so much stronger than he is? Georgie wonders.

"We're doing this the good old-fashioned way," she tells him.

She takes his penis in her hand and pulls it to her. He is powerless; he is drawn inside her, an ocean in an underwater cave. It is good, he thinks, good clean fun. In a moment he erupts. Shuddering, he withdraws.

Claudia pouts, and then proceeds to feel herself up, finish herself off under the blast of the shower. She shivers, moaning, and then gasps. Her back flattens against the wall, her knees buckle.

Georgie watches as his semen drips slowly from the tangled red orgy of her pubic hair. Too slowly. No condom, his mind screams at him. Wake up, you crazy fuck. What if she gets pregnant?

At the thought of bringing a child into this world, Georgie collapses, striking his head hard on the way down, hard against the shower wall.

(Poor Georgie. So much wealth, so little else.)

Georgie wakes up again, for the fourth time that day. At least, he thinks it is still the same day. He is in his bed, in clean fresh sheets. Claudia is stretched out beside him. For a moment, Georgie imagines that they are the happy couple, living the American Dream. Claudia rolls over and grins at him. Compared to that woman, that creature *(don't think about the creature)*, her face is smooth and beautiful. Her body is near flawless. Georgie loves her, her whole self, even the part that hurts him *(especially the part that hurts him)*. Her eyes glow as he looks into them, into her inner life.

"I love you," Georgie says. He says it out loud. He feels the words transform his soul. Everything is different now. Everything is better now.

"I know," Claudia whispers. She smiles at him; she shines with the dying sun, which sets behind her. "Do you think we made a baby?" she whispers.

Georgie feels the weakness overcome him again. His limbs go limp. But it is not so bad, this time. He can take the thought, this time. He can live with it. He turns his head at her snicker. Claudia lifts his limp hand high in the air. She drops it onto the bed. It strikes the mattress with a hollow, woody sound. Claudia rolls swiftly to her side and reaches over the side of the bed. When she comes up, she is holding a thick piece of rope in her hand.

"Stay still," she whispers, as she ties his hands together and then his feet.

Georgie would fight, if he could. No. No, he wouldn't. His arms and legs are weak bags of flesh. His mind, his heart, his soul *(his son?)* belong to Claudia now. He can't muster the will to fight her any more than he could develop the strength in his limbs.

His will is hers now.

She hefts him onto a flat, wooden dolly that lies beside the bed. There is a jump rope tied around it. To Georgie, she looks like an adorable little girl, tugging a little red wagon around the yard. She is probably just playing a game, he thinks. She hauls Georgie down the hallway and then shoves the dolly down the stairs. It bounces and bangs against the hard steps. Georgie's body is jostled and tossed. He slams hard into the banister, breaking his nose. He cries out, feeling the blood spurt; he wants to touch his face, to protect himself, but he is still tied to the dolly, falling helplessly down the stairs. He wants to stop, to cover his head, but his hands are tied behind his back.

As he strikes the downstairs landing, his shoulder takes the full force of his fall. With a snap he feels it dislocate. He screams in pain, screams again and again; he is still screaming as Claudia comes up to him, straps him more tightly onto the dolly.

"That wasn't so bad, was it?" she says brightly. Then she drags him into the back yard.

Georgie wakes up *(for the fifth time that day, if it is still the same day)* to a heavy thud then a softer pitter-patter of something striking wood above his head.

He is in a dark place—a pitch-black place. His breath shudders raggedly in and out. Georgie rolls over and onto something hard that will not budge. He tries to sit up but knocks his head on the same hard substance. He falls back, groaning, panting. Another thud, then that pattering noise echoes overhead. Georgie screams. The bitch is burying him alive.

When Georgie wakes up *(for the sixth time that day, if it is still the same day),* he is covered in pain. His body is bruised and battered, his hands and fingernails throb, and he is panting frantically. Georgie remembers that he is in a coffin. He doesn't remember where the pain came from. For a moment, he recalls a wild thrashing, a panicked horror *(don't think about it).* OK. The thud of dirt falling on top of his coffin continues relentlessly, but it's no longer the insistent noise he remembers. Rather, it is more a vibration that he can feel coming from the earth around his coffin, reverberating in the wood walls.

Georgie inhales deeply. There is not enough air, he thinks desperately. He begins to pant again. I'm going to die down here, he thinks. Fear and peace rush over him in successive waves. Death will be better, anything will be better than this, he thinks. Georgie relaxes into the dizziness that threatens to overcome him; he rides it like a pro, daring nausea to join him. It doesn't. Georgie circles the borders of a vast, dark whirlpool. The force of it lashes his mind with a cool terror. In the center is a splash of light, a tiny, brilliant white speck. Hell would be better than this, he thinks, sighing softly.

Down and down Georgie spins, down towards the beautiful speck. It beckons to him. He hears a slight giggle. He can't see himself, but he is smiling. When he reaches the light, it winks over him. It swallows him whole, and he is nothing.

Dear Diary:

To the best of my ability, to be mindful, watching everything that happens around and to involve myself with that which happens when my life journey is a part of the overall experience.

Damned if You Do

Georgie gasps and air floods his lungs. It stings and burns. The life of it rushes through his skin, setting every nerve fiber tingling. Georgie moans then coughs. He is overcome with another mighty gasp.

"Oh God, oh shite," Claudia weeps. She huddles over him, cradling his head in her lap. She wipes her mouth with the back of her hand. "I'm so sorry, I'm so sorry, Georgie!" She clasps him tightly to her. "I'm so glad you came back," she whispers.

"Wha-what?" Georgie chokes out.

Then he remembers.

"Look at you," Claudia sobs. She caresses his elbows and wrists, gently running her fingers over the bruises and open sores. "I really hurt you."

"You almost died. You did die. You were dead," she explains. "For a minute." Her eyes are wet with tears. "I had to give you CPR."

Georgie places a hand on his head and sits up. He has a headache.

She grabs him in an embrace that he is too weak to shake off.

Christ, what a day.

"I'll never do it again," Claudia sobs. "I promise. I'll never hurt you again. I love you, Georgie. I'm sorry I didn't say it before. I love you. I love you. I love you."

She bursts into fresh sobs. Georgie looks away from her disdainfully. What a spectacle this woman is. How dramatic. He holds his head with both hands.

"It's fine," he groans, in the hope that she will just be quiet. She throws her arms around him, once more.

"It's not fine," she gasps. "But I'll show you. I'll prove to you that you can trust me. I'll never hurt you again."

She begins to kiss his neck, his jaw, running her tongue along his ear lobe. Georgie's penis rises weakly to the challenge. It is tired, sure, but just maybe. Georgie grabs at Claudia's chest.

"Oh Georgie!" she cries, giving herself up to him. "Let's make love. Let's make real love, the way that normal people do. I'm so tired of hurting you."

She gasps as Georgie's penis pokes hard against her. In a moment, she rips off her pants and straddles him on the lawn. Georgie wonders what the neighbors will think, then remembers that Claudia's one of the neighbors. He tries to hide his smile.

"Please, let's just be like a normal couple," Claudia begs, moaning as she rides him. "You wouldn't have to pay me or anything."

Georgie flips her over and mounts her from above. He pumps away inside her, willing her to shut up.

"Oh Georgie, oh Georgie!" Claudia cries. She is nearing orgasm, and so is he.

At the crucial moment, Georgie pulls out of her. Claudia gasps and moans plaintively, reaching for him. He dances out of her reach, then releases, splashing his wad over her toes.

"Mmm," Georgie hums as he finishes off the final spurt.

"Georgie," Claudia whines.

He chuckles. "How about, 'no'?" he suggests. Then he turns and leaves her, naked and yearning, on the lawn.

A few days later, Georgie and Claudia have nurtured their bruised egos and are back to business as usual. Claudia is giving Georgie small cuts on his arm with a chef's knife as she prepares dinner. There is a knock on the door. Georgie rolls down his sleeves and answers it.

"Georgie!" Margaret screeches. "I'm so glad that you're feeling better."

Georgie is bewildered. He wonders if Margaret knows about the old lady in the stone cottage or his being buried alive.

Margaret sees his confusion and greets it with a slight smile. "Is Claudia here?" she says in a low voice.

Georgie nods and opens the door wider. Margaret peeks in and sees Claudia, who waves a knife cheerfully from the kitchen.

"Oh, I've interrupted your dinner," Margaret says, her voice reflecting disappointment. "Perhaps I should come back at a better time?"

Georgie hems and haws for a moment.

"Of course not," Claudia finally yells from the kitchen. "Why don't you stay for dinner?"

"Uh, s-sure," Margaret stutters. "Just let me make a phone call."

Only a short time later, Claudia, Georgie, and Margaret all sit down before a roast chicken, frozen vegetables, and a homemade fruit salad.

"So Margaret, what have you been up to lately?" Claudia says.

Margaret proceeds to tell Claudia about her book deal and the progress she has made. Claudia nods and asks insightful, thoughtful questions, charming as can be. Meanwhile, she slips her foot under the table and applies strong pressure to Georgie's testicles.

"Ow. Oh," Georgie stifles a moan as the pain washes over him.

"Are you ok?" Margaret asks, looking at him with concern.

"Fine," Georgie squeaks. "How do you like the fruit salad?"

"Oh, it's great. Claudia, you're such a good cook," Margaret says. She smiles at them both.

"You know, I have a great idea," she continues after an awkward minute. "I was planning to go to a play with a friend of mine tonight . . . my girlfriend, actually. Would you guys like to come as well? It should be a really good show."

"Um," Georgie looks at Claudia, wondering if going to a play would interfere with whatever nastiness she has planned for him tonight. She nods imperceptibly. Public humiliation it is, Georgie thinks.

"I think that would be great," Georgie says. "We don't get out much these days. And I can't believe I still haven't met your girlfriend."

The four of them—Georgie, Margaret, Claudia, and Mandy—pull up outside the auditorium just before the play is about to begin and slide into their seats as the lights dim, jostling a few people in the process. The complaints silence as the stage lights up.

A man, dressed shabbily, walks onto the stage; a cringing, frightened-looking woman follows close behind. The man stands in the center of the stage in the halo of the spotlight.

"I thought I'd never be free of her," the man announces to the audience, sneering at the woman behind him. "Every moment of every day I would turn around, and there she'd be." He pauses.

"That's what they call love," he announces, and then spits on the stage near the woman's feet.

The audience rustles uneasily.

"And then . . . And then . . . when she told me that she'd gotten pregnant . . . ."

The woman rubs her belly, gazing on it tenderly.

"Well, I knew it had to end right then. I mean me, a father? I can't even take care of myself."

The woman looks up at him, pleading, shaking her head.

"But how to do it?" the man continues, ignoring her. "I'd tried before, and yet she always found me again, always wormed her way back into my life."

The man's face transforms into a hideous mask, with a snarling that appears to hate the world.

"There is only one way," he concludes.

"Death," the woman wails.

The stage lights drop and, when they light up again, the scene is of an exotic, Middle Eastern marketplace, filled with bright splashes of red fabric and chains of gold. The man strides onto the stage, accompanied by a different woman. Behind them follows the cringing, terrified woman–child of before.

The man and his new woman peruse the marketplace. With a grand gesture, he buys her a beautiful necklace. She protests for a moment then accepts it with glee. As she wraps it around her neck, the man steps forward.

"Even before we'd met, she was with me, following me around," he accuses, pointing a finger at the cringing woman, who tries to hide herself behind a rack of shawls.

In the next scene, the man is wandering through his neighborhood in a bathrobe, seeking the woman he bought the necklace for. The woman is nowhere to be seen. The cringing woman appears.

The man is surprised, but not unhappy.

"Hey, why not?" he figures. "It really couldn't hurt to give her a try."

The man and the woman make love in the bathroom. They eat at a fancy restaurant. They dance on the beach together. They fall in love, as people do, with pleasant dates and just enough similarities to get along, just enough differences to keep things interesting.

As the play continues, the man and the cringing woman grow close. They begin to depend on one another. They love each other, in their way, but the man is always pushing her away, and she is always clinging too tight. She wants to move in, but he needs his space. She wants to cuddle, but he has an early meeting.

He doesn't have an early meeting. He actually likes to cuddle. But the thought of actually giving in, of giving her what she wants . . . . The thought twists something deep inside of him, and he must refuse.

Soon, they are both entwined in a relationship that makes them miserable, which transforms them into creatures they no longer recognize, no longer love, but without whom they'd die.

"I love her and hate her," the man says. "I know there's someone better for me, but I'm trapped."

The woman he bought the necklace for appears from time to time. The man yearns for her; he can't get enough of her. He practically begs her to stay with him, to supplant his cringing, loving girlfriend. He buys her extravagant gifts, always greets her with a pleasant smile—a smile his girlfriend never sees. But in the end, his dream woman always escapes. Maybe she sees beyond his superficial charm, or maybe she's just too much a will-o-the-wisp to stay too long in one place.

That is what makes her the perfect dream woman—her perfect distance. The promise that her perfection will never be marred by the machinations of the man's filthy soul. She knows that's what makes her perfect. She loves that she can ensure his yearning by constantly avoiding him. In this way, she feels the satisfaction of being loved without the responsibility.

Georgie, Claudia, and Margaret watch the play in horrible discomfort, afraid to be who they really they think they are, never completely confessing to themselves how much they can relate to the characters.

I'm not really like that, they think, all at one time or another. I'm not.

One night, the man onstage meets his dream woman at a bar. They are both there by accident, and alone. And she has already had a drink . . . or five. She is alone in a bar, as she is heartbroken after yet another failed relationship with another failed man. The perfect woman lets down her guard. She lets the man buy her a drink.

"It's been too damn long," she mutters into her tequila. She looks at the man accusingly. "You ever go three months without a lay?" she demands.

He grins. Shakes his head. Lays his hand on the small of her back.

"A gorgeous woman like you?" he says softly. "I hardly believe it."

She scoffs.

"You must be punishing yourself," he whispers. "You don't need to punish yourself."

Her hungry lips reach up to touch his. They meet, tequila churning like fire in their bellies. In moments, they are tearing each other's clothes off in her apartment. They can't even wait to move to the bedroom. He pushes her against a wall and shoves into her, hard.

She loves it.

The perfect woman likes it rough.

The next morning, racked with guilt, the dream woman confesses to the cringing girlfriend, who is five months' pregnant with the man's child.

"I didn't mean to," she begs. "I was drunk, and he was . . . I never thought we would." Her voice drops to a whisper, her face ashamed. "Please forgive me."

"Forgive you?" the girlfriend sobs. "What's to forgive? It's him—that bastard! You were single, after all. It was his choice to break my trust."

Together they wail their heartbreak.

"I've tried to leave him, so many times," the girlfriend says, shuddering, "but he always draws me back in, you know?"

The dream woman stares at her with wide eyes. "I know exactly what you mean."

In the final moment, their bond of shared grief gives way. In a fit of madness and jealousy, the cringing woman knocks the dream woman down and beats her with a thick, phallic-shaped paperweight. "He loves me," she screams. "He does. He will always love me."

Coming upon the gory scene, the man strangles his cringing girlfriend. "You killed her—my dreams and my hope," he screeches. When she is limp in his arms he tosses her corpse to the floor.

Then a hideous look floods his face. "My son," he whispers. "You killed him, too."

Sinking to his knees, he weeps. And when he stops, the man slowly climbs onto a chair and hangs himself with a piece of wire, laughing and sobbing all at once.

"Well, that was a trip!" Mandy gushes as they exit the theater. "Can you believe that? Where do they come up with this stuff?"

Georgie becomes intensely interested in a poster on the wall, while Margaret and Claudia exchange a desperate glance and then look away, embarrassed. Claudia wonders if Margaret ever would sleep with Georgie. Margaret is wondering the same thing. She hopes that Claudia doesn't believe it of her. She wonders whether Claudia would kill her, if she had reason to.

"I think the ending was a little unrealistic," Margaret says, with hollow laughter. She glances over quickly at Claudia to see if she agrees.

Claudia stares blankly, not listening. She is thinking of the cringing woman—how much she hates her.

I'm not that woman, she decides. I'm in control of this situation. I am the tormentor. Georgie's the one—he's the one who can't live without *me*. He wants *me*. He loves me. He told me so.

Claudia briefly considers getting a new job, but for some reason she can't hold onto the idea in her head for more than half a second.

"Well?" Mandy says. She looks up at both Claudia and Margaret and then searches for Georgie. "What's wrong with you guys?" she mumbles.

Claudia scrutinizes Georgie, watching as he scans the poster on the wall. She wonders how the play has affected him. How worried is he? She starts thinking about how she can drive the knife in even more deeply.

Dear Diary:

To the best of my ability, to let go of my attachments, to all circumstances, outcomes and consequences.

Hunting They Will Go

Several weeks pass. Claudia watches Georgie as he mopes around, and wonders when the time will be ripe for twisting in that knife. She takes a break from the torture, gives him time to heal—time to become complacent. She still burns him now and then and, sometimes, she brings out the whip and chains—just to keep him on his toes—but that's just child's play. Not the real deal. Not true torture. Claudia slides into a bit of a slump, weighing her jealousy against her job—and her satisfaction of destroying Georgie—against her own possible pain. They hear nothing from Margaret. Claudia hopes the play scared Margaret enough to keep her away from Georgie—forever. Finally, Claudia climbs out of the slump; she works through her reaction to the play, and when she becomes just crazy enough to go through with it, Claudia speaks.

"Georgie," Claudia says in a soft, slightly singsong tone.

Georgie looks up at her. Her eyes are wide and glimmering.

"I was talking to Margaret earlier," she begins. This is a lie, but she says it anyway. "We were thinking it would be fun for the four of us to take a trip—you, me. Margaret. Mandy. What do you think?"

It doesn't sound horrible. That's what Georgie thinks. After all, things with Claudia have been pretty nice lately. Except . . .

"Where?" he asks.

"Well, you know that cabin your parents own? Out on the lake?"

Georgie doesn't think he ever told Margaret about the cabin and this trip is probably all Claudia's idea. A nagging doubt begins to creep in.

"We were thinking," Claudia says, "that it would be a nice opportunity to get away, try something new. I mean, Georgie, you and I haven't spent one single night away from this house. Not together. Not once since I moved in."

Claudia's expression is very clear: 'No' will be an unacceptable answer. Georgie wonders how bad a trip away could be, trying hard to ignore the strong possibility that it could be very bad indeed. Very, very bad.

"Yeah, sure," he says, "sounds like fun."

Claudia squeals. "Oh, Georgie, thank you!" She gives him a hug, and proceeds to bounce around like a little girl. "Oh, it's going to be so much fun. You are not going to regret this."

Georgie thinks that he is going to regret this a great deal; he sighs and rolls his eyes. She's probably planning on skinning him alive and hanging him upside down from a tree. Yet, at this point, Georgie is beyond caring. After everything Claudia's put him through, he can't imagine her hurting any more than she already has.

And still that nagging doubt: Maybe, as they say, he hasn't seen anything yet.

They decide to leave the weekend after next even though Mandy won't be able to come. Instead, Margaret invites her friend Carl, just one more man, like Georgie, who wants desperately to fuck Margaret, and never will.

On the morning they leave, both Carl and Georgie fight to hold the limo door open for Margaret and, as they continue with the macho positioning—the huffing and puffing and kicking up dirt, Margaret goes to the other side of the limo where Ben is holding the door open for everyone. Claudia sniffs derisively and crawls in after Margaret.

"Men," she says, rolling her eyes.

"Oh, I know." Margaret giggles, lowering her voice, "That's why I prefer women, you know."

She winks. Claudia smiles awkwardly.

Georgie and Carl finally get the door open. They settle down, but not before grunting, snorting, and clearing their throats. Then Ben puts his foot to the gas pedal, and they're on their way.

Ben drops the four off at the cabin, then reverses the limo and backs down the road. Georgie watches him drive away, not sure where Ben stays and not sure he cares either.

The "cabin" is more a mansion. Rising three stories among the trees, rows of gabled windows greet the travelers. The front entrance is surrounded by a massive deck adorned with the thick trunks of two spruce trees, which form giant columns and cast shadows on the door.

Claudia pulls a roll of mints out of her purse, offers one to Georgie as they walk together towards the front entry. Georgie shrugs, and takes it, not noticing that she doesn't take one herself. He knows that when someone offers you a breath mint, you should take it.

He wonders if she's offered the breath mint because she plans on fucking him soon; the idea cheers him significantly. Sex with Claudia has not been half bad lately. He pops the white strip into his mouth, and it quickly dissolves.

For the next half hour, Georgie gives everyone a tour of the cabin, shows them to their rooms, and points out the few walking paths around the lake. He shows Carl how to start the generator, and then the two men flop down onto a soft and well-used sofa as Claudia and Margaret unpack coolers and put food in the refrigerator.

Georgie and Carl stare at each other with intense hostility for about 15 minutes until Georgie becomes distracted by a fly buzzing against the window.

"Georgie?" Margaret's voice seems to fill the room around him, echoing off the walls. "Georgie," she repeats, "are you okay?"

Georgie stares at her; her cheeks seem swollen.

"I'm fine," he answers, his voice coming from somewhere very far away.

"Be cool," Georgie thinks. "Be very very cool, cool, cool, cool." His tongue begins to feel like it's crowding his mouth, taking up too much room, crowded against the roof of his mouth. He looks over at Claudia. She looks just as evil as always. Georgie decides not to look at her anymore. Instead, he looks down at a plate full of spaghetti and wonders when it became dinnertime and when he sat down at the table and when he even moved from the living room to the dining room. He doesn't remember any of it, and he doesn't understand why his spaghetti is moving, undulating, and swirling uncontrollably on his plate.

(Parenthetical Pet Peeve) When people take food off my plate without asking.

Georgie laughs.

"There's a black hole in my spaghetti," he announces.

"What?" Carl asks peevishly, which doesn't surprise Georgie. Carl strikes him as a peevish man in general. A bit of a complainer, Georgie thinks; he watches as Carl glances at Claudia, who shrugs.

Georgie snorts. "You don't see it?" he asks, pointing at his still swirling spaghetti. "You're missing out . . ."

Margaret gets to her feet and crosses the room to Georgie's side of the table and places a hand on his forehead.

"Are you sure you're okay?" she asks. The worry in her voice is unmistakable.

"Weird," Georgie says. "I'm feeling a little weird." He looks up at her with hope, and with love shining brightly through his eyes. He pushes the love out of his eyes and into her eyes. If he does it just right, she will love him back. Georgie knows that, just as he knows that he's not sure he knows how to do anything right. And what if she doesn't love him back? What then?

A loud, rumbling thump distracts him. His spaghetti trembles in fear. An earthquake? A low-flying jet? No.

It is Claudia's fist on the table.

"Georgie—orgy orgy orgy orgy," she says. "Behave yourself for once."

"You're not my mom," he says. He sticks his tongue out at her.

Is Claudia his mom? What if Claudia is his mom? If Claudia is his mom, then he is Claudia's son. No—his mom is just a stupid, old fat lady who can't speak proper English, and has a drinking problem. That's his mom. Not Claudia. But . . . If Claudia is like his mom is (or was), then any minute now she will leave, or she will come to him crying, wearing that pink silk, lace-trimmed nightgown she bought when she was just a chubby—not fat—old lady. That nightgown that doesn't fit her, hasn't fit her in years, so tight that her breasts are always spilling out of it, taunting Georgie. Such big, untouchable breasts. Breasts he shouldn't see. Shouldn't think about.

(So don't. Don't think about them, Georgie.

Okay, he answers dutifully.)

Margaret speaks. Georgie watches her mouth move but can't hear the words she says—the words that mean she loves Georgie. Has always loved Georgie and always will love Georgie. Georgie basks in the attention, the love he feels entering every pore, setting afire every nerve. It is good to be loved by Margaret, to be treasured by such a good good person. Still, Georgie wishes he could hear what she's saying.

Claudia speaks now, too, but Georgie's not sure he cares about hearing what Claudia has to say. She loves him; Georgie knows that/senses that, but Claudia hurts him. And, as good as it feels to be loved by Margaret, that's how bad it feels to be loved by Claudia. She's a bad person. Evil even. Her face is covered in dark spots that move, swarm across her face like wasps, stinging. Georgie hopes she's allergic to bug bites and stings. Georgie hopes her throat will close and she will choke. That's what Georgie hopes.

But no. She's not choking. She's talking and laughing, covering her hand with her face.

"Claudia," Georgie says.

"Claudia," he repeats.

Claudia Claudia Claudia. I'm in love with Claudia Nesbitt? Me? In love with Claudia Nesbitt? Me, in love with the woman who hurts me? The one who tortures me? The one whose face is a mask of stinging, swarming wasps?

Georgie tries once more to call her name, but the words don't come, and he finds himself singing, sinking into the couch, the cushions. Someone throws a blanket over him. It's a scratchy blanket; its fibers irritate his arms. The blanket is nothing but scratchy fibers, and so is Georgie. In his mind, the fibers grow through the edges of the blanket and into his skin, burrowing beneath his flesh like a bot fly until Georgie is nothing but blanket, and the blanket is nothing but Georgie. He opens his eyes. They are magical, like camera eyes. *(Lens?)* They zoom in on the ceiling, going in for the close-up. Georgie *is* the lens. He is a convex universe made of glass. The wood grain of the ceiling flows like a river—an unmoving wooden river. Whum, whum, whum. The wood river goes nowhere. Still Georgie wants the wood to flow, to flow like water, up and out, spilling over the dam. Breaking free.

"Georgie Porgie. Georgie Porgie. Georgie Porgie!" Claudia sings. He imagines her with pigtails, like a little girl.

"How are you liking your little nappy-poo, Georgie, baby?" Claudia whispers.

Whum, whum, whum.

Margaret's face appears over the couch. She shines with the light of an angel. Claudia is little more than shadow.

"Is he any better?" someone asks.

"Not yet."

Yet, bet, debt, yeti—

"Should we call a doctor?"

"He'll be fine."

Claudia lays her hand on Margaret's wrist, encircling it with her fingers. Such a dainty wrist, that Margaret—that angel—has.

"It's just an episode," Claudia says.

Claudia—that bitch, that whore, that woman I love and hate. She created a paradise and then set it aflame. She is my world and its end, my kinky sex goddess, my creepy-crawly nemesis. She never stood a chance. I never stood a chance. We love and hate—no matter whose face she's wearing, whose heart she's tearing. I want to see her in those sling-backs; her perverted, cotton-candy blue toes peeking out to play.

A popping noise reminds Georgie to look sideways. There is a glow—a fire—and there are three people sitting around it. Georgie wants to roll over, but that would be too hard. The three pass around a glass bottle filled with a clear substance that sloshes around. They bring it to their lips, taking turns. He knows what it is. Georgie's tongue feels like a piece of felt in his mouth; he wants to move it, but can't. Clear sloshy would be a bad idea anyway. Georgie is in a good place.

Two of the people are girls, and one is a boy. The girls are laughing together. One has bright, fire-like hair. One puts her hand on the other one's leg. Georgie is angry. He remembers that he wants both girls for himself, and he can't have both. He's angry they can have each other. He watches them kiss. The bright fire-like hair glows and blends into the fire. The fire wraps around them both; walls of gorgeous flames surround them. Georgie wants to burn with them. The boy reaches out and touches them both. Georgie wants to be the boy. They all collapse together in front of the fire, and Georgie, watching, is with them, too.

Georgie walks through a doorway into a dark hall.

"Stop right there," a voice commands.

Georgie stops.

"Be careful," the voice continues evilly, seductively. "Or else. You don't want it to get you, do you?"

Georgie hears the heavy panting of some enormous creature. He freezes, terrified. "Hi, Princess," Claudia's voice whispers close to his ear. "Come on in."

Georgie tiptoes sideways to avoid the hole he knows is in the floor beside him—the monster that waits salivating, waits hoping Georgie will misstep. He creeps into the living room, now out of the hallway, where he finds Claudia kissing another woman. It's that Sara girl.

Claudia and Sara stand topless in the center of the room. Claudia is wearing her latex suit. There is a small audience beside Georgie, watching. Greg is mid-50s with long, white hair. He has a potbelly, a fuzzy navel. Georgie tics. Claudia sees Georgie's neck jerk and his eyes roll. She waves him to come closer.

"Just don't come too close—"

The creature in the dark hallway breathes heavily, drooling, just behind Georgie, waiting to devour him. The breathing revs up to a scream—a pulsing wail.

"Don't leave," Claudia shouts.

"Fuck you. I fucking love you," Georgie yells at her. "You're fucking with my mind again."

"I'm not," Claudia insists. "I'm really not. I told you I wouldn't, and I'm not."

The screaming becomes louder, and evolves into a high-pitched screech. Georgie presses his hands against his ears.

"I'm just a habit, Georgie. An addiction."

Claudia soothes him. She tapes his mouth shut and cuffs his wrists to his ankles. He is done for—captive once again. Georgie struggles to break free of his bonds. His shirt slides up and exposes his rounded belly, yet the veins on his neck do not stand out. They are nowhere near the surface. Claudia laughs. Her hair glows like fire as the flames shadow her face. It is dark. Georgie can't see—he can't see anything.

"You disgust me," Claudia whispers. She nibbles at his ear. "You're pathetic."

Georgie screams and yells at her, but his mouth is still taped shut.

"Oh. What's that, Princess?" Claudia simpers. "Are you trying to speak like a real person? Let me help you with that."

Georgie watches Sara caress Claudia's breasts as she rolls down Claudia's latex suit and exposes her fiery bush. Claudia moves away from Sara long enough to shove her shiny red sandals up against Georgie's nose. He inhales deeply and then freezes as the noise resurfaces—that screeching.

"Don't go!" Claudia commands him. His mother leers over him; a flickering candle intermittently lights her face as she clenches a carving knife and fork tightly in her fists. Flames lick at the legs of the chair. Georgie struggles, pulling against his bondage. He pleads to Claudia through the tape on his mouth, but she can't give a fuck.

She cannot care. That's what he's paying her for. Not to care. He's not paying for love. He's paying for hate, for pain, to be ground into nothingness, and waste away in a vast, dark emptiness. Claudia pulls out a condom from Georgie's wallet. She sticks her tongue out at him. She unbuttons his pants, and coughs from the smoke in the air.

Her hair is on fire, too, but it doesn't seem to bother her. Her hair. That's the source of all her power, Georgie realizes. Claudia brings her face close to his crotch and sniffs. Her face distorts, lengthens, until she's no longer human. She's a fox, a coyote. Canine. With dangerous teeth and crafty, clever intelligence. The monster begins to scream and screech, again. The smoke rises around them.

Claudia strips the latex off and stands naked before him. She tears open a condom and bites a hole in it. Laughing, she tosses it at his feet.

"You can't be safe," she snarls. "What's the point of trying, when it always comes back to this?"

Georgie strains, and screams through the tape. He tries to hide, but his penis is pulsing, trying to spring from his pants. He hates her. He wants her.

"What's that, Princess?" Claudia rips the tape off his mouth.

"Fucking whore, bitch, cunt!" Georgie screams.

Claudia laughs.

"Good," she purrs.

Claudia and Sara lie face to crotch, burying their faces between one another's legs, moaning in ecstasy. Georgie wonders if they'll let him join them.

The creature shrieks, breathing down Georgie's neck. "No, no, no," Georgie screams. He's just a little boy, a kid, not strong enough to fight back—only strong enough to know what's going on, know it's wrong, and to be terrified by it. "Leave me alone," something small and alone pleads.

But he can do nothing to stop her. Stop the pleasure. The assault. She is on top of him, riding his erect penis faster and faster. "Get me pregnant, Georgie," she demands. "Give me my fucking love child." She spits in his face.

Georgie shakes his head back and forth, protesting; his entire body shakes in protest. "Cum inside me, Georgie," she hollers. "Cum inside me, you fucking waste of a man. You prepubescent asshole." Her voice, wretched and horrible, rises and evolves into that of screaming alarm. She is evil. Wrinkled and horrible, bent and wicked. She is the crone, the hag. That creature from the forest. They blend, become one. All the women Georgie has ever known. They are one. And he fucks them all.

"Son of a crack whore, bitch, cunt," Georgie screams. And then something deep inside him releases, gives up, explodes into nothingness. He shoots his wad again and again and again. Into every woman he's ever known. For an eternity. His orgasm lasts an eternity, suspends all life around him, he is gone, brought back only by the incessant whine of Claudia's voice:

"I don't love you," she is whispering, shuddering. "I never loved you. I only want to hurt you, make you suffer. Just like you wanted.

Just like you asked me. You—you're not worth it. Not worth anything but pain, and that's what I love, Georgie. Not you. Never you."

The alarm rises overhead, smoke chokes their lungs, and her hair is a vibrating nest of flame—then, pounding on the door. Someone save them!

(Poor, poor Georgie.)

Claudia's face is now peaceful and blue. Her lips open and close slightly; her eyelids are shut, calm, and dreaming. Her hair splashes purple around her head. It moves, swims; it's got a mind of its own— Claudia's hear does. Georgie gets to his feet; he wobbles, nearly trips over her. "Her hair," he thinks. Slowly, he unclenches his fingers, and feels them as blades, and they slide apart. Snip. He cuts and cuts, sliding the blades through every inch of her serpent-like hair, and douses the purple flame. "No, no, no, no, no, no, no, no—" He snips her ear, and her eyes fly wide open, and she screams. The blood seeps out, and forms puddles on the dark, wood, moonbeam-splashed floor. Georgie is screaming too, but he can't hear a sound. And, then, there is nothing; a nothing so deep there is no more room, not even for bliss.

Dear Diary:

To the best of my ability, to know that I am not the cause of others' actions.

Wake Up and Smell the Dopamine

"Georgie," a soft voice calls. His eyes flutter open. The angel stands over him. She breathes gently in his face. She is white, brilliant white, and she overcomes him.

"I'm dead," Georgie realizes. I'm dead and this is heaven.

"Why did you do it, Georgie?" the angel asks softly.

"I didn't mean to," Georgie replies groggily.

(What did I do?

You know what you did.

No. No, I don't.

If you don't know what you did, how do you know you didn't mean to?

Because I never mean anything.

No. You meant to. You know you did.

But, I didn't. You've got to believe me. I didn't mean to.

It was intentional, Georgie. You did it. You meant it.

I thought I wanted it, but I was wrong. Can't a guy be wrong?)

"Claudia," he gasps.

The angel soothes his forehead. "I don't think it's a good idea to see her right now," Margaret says.

"What?"

Margaret shakes her head in sympathy. "Don't you remember, Georgie?"

Georgie remembers the fire, their loving orgy. The fire—

"You cut off Claudia's hair," Margaret whispers. "She's furious."

Georgie laughs.

"Is that all?" he says.

Margaret looks at him sternly.

"A woman's hair is nothing to mess with," she says. "And, what did Claudia do to you, anyway?"

Margaret comes to a realization, and she bites her lip slightly. Georgie laughs again.

"You have no idea," he says. His voice is empty—terrifyingly empty. "I don't even know the worst of it—not yet, anyway."

Georgie, Claudia, Margaret, and Carl slowly climb into the limousine later that day. Georgie has a massive hangover from the drugs Claudia slipped him. Claudia, Margaret, and Carl have hangovers from their own night of revelry. Claudia needs to see a hairstylist to do something about the wreck Georgie left, and, for now, she's not speaking to him, which makes the atmosphere in the limo strained and uncomfortable. The one time he manages to get her alone she hisses at him, like a snake and, when that doesn't work, doesn't make him go away, she slaps his face.

"This, this is not what we agreed on," she snarls, gesturing to her butchered hair.

Later, Ben suppresses a smile as the group silently exits the limo. You could say he's not surprised by how things turned out. You could say that.

Georgie and Claudia drift into their separate worlds over the next few weeks. Georgie returns to his old fetishes, his sicko-twisted paid-for fantasy world. Claudia returns to Greg and Sara. Now that she has a new job, it doesn't matter if she fucks her old boss (and his wife). Actually, if she stops fucking her new boss, she might lose her job. Or get double pay. It is a toss-up, that one—

Georgie returns to the stone cottage on the mountaintop, but there is no one there. He lies on the bearskin rug, his dick limp and useless. Like a boy's. He breathes in the smell of the rug and waits for the disgust to come. He is empty. There is nothing in him anymore—no chords to strike. No emotions to feed off. His life is as boring as he always feared (knew) it would be.

Georgie returns from his empty trip to the cottage, decides he needs groceries then wanders aimlessly up and down the aisles. He's like a ghost waiting for someone to haunt. Someone to scare, to touch. Waiting for something. Anything. Nothing could be worse than this. He scans the sterile shelves crowded with prepackaged food, watches the mouth-breathers who stalk their prey—the Oreo cookies, the Ding Dongs and Twinkies—and who graze on potato chips or Fritos. Sugar or salt. Salt or sugar. The basket shudders uneasily in his hand. It is empty.

From behind he feels movement, then Margaret's voice: "Hey, Georgie." She must have snuck up on him, proving once again that Georgie's no predator; he's prey just like the Ding Dongs and Twinkies.

"Margaret." Relief quiets his poor, angry, tormented brain for one sweet second.

She stares at the floor for a moment, clutching a package of bargain bulk cereal to her chest. Georgie knows that she is thinking of the cabin, of how she saw him: the town fool, an utter idiot. Georgie knows, she's been playing it over in her mind, trying to make sense of, wondering if she saw what she knows she saw. (Everything.)

"I know that you didn't find your nanny," she says finally. She looks up at him, eyes glistening. "I know that you didn't because you're not any better. If anything, you're worse."

Georgie nods. There's no use disagreeing with her.

"So," she says, "I did some research. And the thing is, Georgie, I found her. I found her for you."

She drops her head and rummages through her purse, eventually pulling out a piece of paper. Georgie thinks about her skin as she presses the paper into his hand.

Margaret steps closer to him. She is in the small cloud of heat his body emits. Her hair smells like flowers. She looks up into his face, begging.

"Go see her, Georgie," she says. "Please. If not for me, then for yourself."

He rubs the scrap of paper between two fingers. He stares doubtfully at Margaret. She notices.

"You have to see her," Margaret says. "It's the only way."

"The only way what?" Georgie says.

Margaret looks at him reluctantly. "The only way for you to get better."

Georgie looks down at the paper. If he rubs the ink away, it will be impossible for him to find her. It will be like she never existed, like before.

He squints at Margaret. Accusing her.

"Why do you care? Whether I'm better or not, it's none of your concern."

"I'm your friend, Georgie."

He snorts at her. "You and your one-hit wonders." He glowers, face distorted. "You think a trip to the Dalai Lama, a visit to my old nanny, and a self-help book are gonna make all my problems disappear?"

Georgie holds the note up to her face. "What's next, Margaret? A magician? More doctors?" He grips the paper in both hands, threatening to tear it. "Ever think that maybe I don't want to get better, don't want to believe in all the bullshite people tell themselves to pretend they're happy? Huh, Margaret? Ever think of that?"

(Is that it, Ben? Is it that you don't even want to heal?

Is that what you call it? Healing? Hell, doc, I don't know . . .

Because if you don't, if you really don't want to get better, then why do you keep coming to see me, Ben?

I don't know, Dr C. You're the doctor. Why don't you tell me?)

Margaret's eyes are full of tears, and yet . . . Behind those tears is a fierceness Georgie's never seen. "I care about you," she finally says. "Even if you don't."

Georgie looks at the slip of paper in his hands.

"More bullshite," he mutters. "Love, healing. It's all bullshite."

"Then it's bullshite, Georgie." Margaret turns, walks away from him, leaving him to wonder if she's leaving for good, if she'll stop being his friend if he doesn't get better, if he doesn't want to get better.

"It's too hard," he wants to scream.

Dear Diary:

In general, to the best that I am able, I need to get over it, no matter what the "it" might be.

Then, Unto Them

Claudia drags herself out of her old beater of a station wagon and leans against it, staring at the dull, gray building before her. The parking lot seems to stretch in front of her like something only Escher could have imagined. Her tender breasts scream at her as they push against her bra, against the fabric of her shirt. She reaches inside the car and bends—carefully and slowly—to pick up her purse from the passenger's seat and is overcome with another wave of nausea. She retches silently, grateful nothing comes out, and then with a dogged determination staggers up the walk to the clinic. Whatever Georgie planted inside her is pure evil, as it's eating her alive, and it's got to be removed.

She has missed Georgie in some sick and twisted way. She contemplates the cottage, and also missing Greg and Sara so at least for now, she's back at the home she thinks she should call home, puttering around Georgie's house, again. A mug of warm water and lemon in her hands, she sips at it slowly, squeezing her eyes shut. She tries to pretend that it is coffee.

It is not. It never was. It never could be.

(Why doesn't she just make some coffee?

Shh, doc. Give the girl a minute, would you? She's back. I've brought her back, doc. See? I'm just not there. I am the observer now.)

And so, with Georgie away, seeing his psychiatrist, Claudia stands in front of the living room window and stares out at the view—at the narrow strip of grass between Georgie's house and the sidewalk, the carefully trimmed ficus trees, the hydrangea, and across the street is her still, burned-down house. It's an eyesore. But eventually, she knows, the insurance will come through, and she'll move back, move on, and move out. How long does she stand there, staring at the unchanging view? Finally, she gives up, moves to the kitchen, the window above the sink. A different view. One of the side street but still the same carefully trimmed ficus trees, the overgrown hydrangea. Window to window, Claudia moves, hoping for/expecting a different view, unique somehow, and when she doesn't find it, she collapses on the sofa in the living room, cradling her stomach.

She doesn't feel well and, for today, she has given up food. What's the point, after all? Claudia thinks about the how, the why, and she doesn't worry about Georgie. She worries about herself; she presses gently on her belly, trying to keep it all in. Trying to prevent anything from getting back out.

(Wait. Is she?)

She brings her hand to her mouth, belching. Oh, this isn't good. This isn't good, at all. No. She can feel the bile rising, jumps from the sofa, and runs to the bathroom. Not again. Claudia collapses against the toilet, retching again and again. There is nothing left, nothing but a little bit of lemon water. She brings that up as well. To the uninformed observer, it looks like little more than vomiting, but for those who know, who understand, it's clear that Claudia is ridding herself of every rotten thing she has ever done to Georgie—the times she humiliated him, hurt him, the time she twisted his pinky until the knuckle broke, the time she buried him . . . . What was she thinking?

Claudia sobs and hiccoughs; she belches, vomits again. She always knew it would come back to haunt her, didn't she? It was only a matter of time.

When Georgie comes home, she is standing in the hall waiting for him. The corners of her mouth are crusted with vomit; her eyes look haunted and tired. To Georgie, she looks like some ghoulish version of her older self. He stares at her, walks toward her to engulf her in his arms—she looks like she could use a hug—and steps in a splash of vomit. He is completely repulsed, can think only of getting the puke off his shoes. He steps back away from her, and again slides. Jesus. He can feel his stomach begin to heave.

(Parenthetical Pet Peeve) Shoes with 6-foot long laces that constantly keep untying themselves.

"Georgie," Claudia cries, "Are you okay? Don't fall."

She reaches for him, but Georgie withdraws. He's never been good with sick people.

"Georgie," she sobs, "Georgie, I'm pregnant."

She falls dramatically at his feet, her shoulders shaking with silent tears. Years from now, Georgie will wonder if he did the wrong thing, if there was anything he could have done to make it right, but for now all he can think is to get away from this woman—this woman who reeks of vomit and self-loathing.

He stares at her, huddled on the floor, her arm snaking towards his feet. "Get up," he tells her.

She remains motionless, glued to the spot. Georgie glances at her, then lifts one foot, staring at the sole of his shoe, streaked with the remnants of Claudia, her vomit, and her disgrace. Her shame. He can't figure out the best way to erase that shame, without touching the vomit. He's perplexed. Maybe he'll have to wear these shoes forever.

Claudia moves, slithers toward him, tugging at his pants.

"Georgie," she whispers. "What are we going to do?"

"Is it mine?" he asks.

Claudia hangs her head.

"It isn't, is it?" he says.

She says nothing for such a long time that Georgie loses track of what he's asked, his mind drifting back to the shoe issue. These are his Hugo Boss loafers, the ones he likes to wear without socks, the ones he's had for years. The Hugo Bosses are his favorite loafers. His favorite shoes of all the shoes he's ever had in his entire life, and now they're dirty. Smeared with vomit. Ruined. Because of Claudia, who still lies unmoving at his feet.

She stares up at him, pleading. "I don't know," she finally says. "I don't know whose it is."

But Georgie, by now, has completely dismissed her and her "problem"; it's none of his concern. She's the one pregnant, not him. He's got more important problems—his shoes—and now, at last, his mind is beginning to work, beginning to solve the problem. He remembers the hose curled in the front yard, tucked neatly beneath the hydrangea. Claudia now forgotten, Georgie races back out of the house and down the stairs, pulls out the hose, then balancing perfectly on one leg and looking a bit like a flamingo, Georgie begins hosing off his shoes.

He is meticulous, methodical. He stands first on his right leg, lifts his left foot, and hoses down the sole; then he stands on his left leg and repeats the process. He is pleased that he has figured out the problem, come up with the solution. Except . . .

Except now . . . Except now that he thinks about it, how can he be sure that the vomit is only on the soles? How can he know for certain that nothing splashed on the top of his Hugo Bosses? Truth is, he can't. So he hoses off the tops then starts wondering whether anything splashed on his jeans, hoses them off as well and his shirt, while he's at it. And then, to be doubly safe, he hoses down his hair, his face, every last part of himself, until he is standing in the middle of the front yard, dripping wet.

And still . . . it's not enough. There could be vomit on the porch, on the windows, anywhere, and then, feeling like a fireman, he turns the hose on the house, washing away the stench of vomit, the chunks he knows that Claudia's left behind.

Bitch.

Finished washing his own house clean, he turns his attention to the burned-out lot where Claudia's house once stood. He aims his hose at the lot, flooding the ash, scattering it to reveal even more ash.

He thinks about Claudia's house, what it must have been like to live there, how it must have felt like for Claudia walking room to room, what it feels like now knowing she'll never have another chance to walk room to room. Not in the same house. And then he starts wondering if she's still stretched out on his hall floor. She shouldn't be. He wants her gone. She should know that, and he wonders if she does know that he wants her gone. Then he wonders—worries—that maybe she's still puking, getting his floor greasy with vomit, and he wonders if the hose will reach inside, let him clean the hall floor, the whole fucking house. Washing it clean of Claudia.

Or maybe he'll just wash her down with the hose. Hose off all those freckles, hose down all those curls. The spray would be so fast, so hard it would knock her senseless, push her back against the wall. He sees it—her body being blown apart, pieces flying—one arm in the kitchen, the other draped over the lamp in the living room; a leg in the hall, a foot on the porch. And her head . . . Her head in the attic where all heads belong. There is a precision to it.

No, Georgie thinks, that's not how it would work. She'd stay intact. There'd be no body parts flying, but the water—so hard, so fast—would dig into her, cut a hole through her belly until he could see right through. Or maybe no hole in her belly. Maybe the water would just wash away her color, her skin until she was completely translucent. A holy creature. He snickers: Claudia, holy? Claudia, clean?

The water in the hose begins to sputter and with one final spurt has run out completely. No more water. None at all. The hose is flat. Georgie turns around. Claudia is waiting for him, her hand on the spigot.

"Well?" she asks. He walks close to her. Her eyes are still haunted, stained with tears. Her face is old and wrinkled; her chin sags, and her hair still has flecks of vomit in it. In all seriousness, who could love this woman?

"What are we going to do, Georgie?" she asks.

I don't know, I don't know, I don't know!

(I do.)

"Do whatever you want," he tells her. "I don't care."

She looks at him. Slowly, oh slowly, her eyes begin to narrow. Like mountains forming, her face becomes an angry, bitter mask.

"Fuck you, Georgie," she spits. "Fuck you hard. Right up the ass."

Her eyes glow red.

(How does she make them do that?)

"Just go fuck yourself," she says, raising her chin, daring him to hit it. "I don't need this shite."

Dear Diary:

I wish I could have the courage to abandon myself from all of my obsessions.

Claudia Moves Out

Georgie shuffles through the house, hating every wall, every window, every tile, every everything. He hates it. Everywhere he turns he sees Claudia. Here she strung him up; there she burned him with cigarette butts. Over in the chair she cut him. In the bathroom she drowned him. On the porch, she humiliated him, time and again.

Numb now, Georgie wonders how he ever thought he was bored with Claudia. With her, life was a torturous show, a jagged-toothed adventure. Without her, he is back to making thermoses of 10-shot espresso. It does nothing for him—doesn't give him jitters or clear his head, doesn't jumpstart him in any way. It's Claudia fault. Without her, nothing jumpstarts him anymore. He wants her back.

His days are endless, ceaseless. If he had the nerve, he'd end it all. Instead, he pounds coffee, smokes, does his laundry now and then, and goes shopping.

(Parenthetical Pet Peeve) Public laundromats that leave your clothes still wet after two hours of drying time.

Georgie roams the aisles of the grocery store, searching for Margaret or the perfect snack food or a two-for-one sale on cigarettes. Nothing comes of his endless searching, but Georgie—the eternal optimist—thinks maybe tomorrow or the day after, he'll walk these aisles and there in Aisle 7 will be Margaret buying the perfect snack, and she'll smile at him and tell him the store is having that two-for-one sale on cigarettes, and he better hurry before someone else buys out the entire supply.

Maybe.

It could happen. Georgie knows what people say—that truth is stranger than fiction, so he wanders the aisles, waiting for tomorrow to come, for Margaret to show, for his cigarettes to go on sale. He wanders for so long—nearly $3^1/_2$ hours—that the clerks and cashiers begin to notice him, and begin following close behind him.

Maybe I should have changed, Georgie thinks. Maybe wearing my robe to the store wasn't such a great idea. It makes him noticeable, and Georgie doesn't want to be noticeable.

"Can I help you?"

Georgie looks around, alarmed to discover that a tall, stooped man, in a crisp white shirt, red vest, and gabardine pants, was talking to him. He looks like a store manager, Georgie thinks, wondering if a store manager has any kind of legal authority.

"Excuse me," the man says again, "but are you looking for something in particular?"

The man knows Georgie's not looking for anything in particular, and Georgie knows the man—the manager—knows that Georgie knows. And still the man persists in asking. People are a mystery to Georgie. He stares into the man's face, and for the briefest of seconds, the man's face seems to melt, to morph into Claudia's, and Georgie begins to panic; he can feel the breath catch in his throat, the sweat drip down his face.

"Sir," the man asks, "Are you all right? Do you need help?"

What is it with strangers always asking if he needs help and Claudia—that bitch, that whore—never once asking? What is love if not offering help? Claudia never loved him.

"Sir," the man repeats.

Georgie blinks, deciding he's had an epiphany although he's not absolutely sure what an epiphany is.

"No," he tells the man in the vest. "I don't need help. Just tell me, is it true your cigarettes are on sale this lovely day?"

Five short minutes later, a stocky, young woman wearing a blood-spattered apron holds Georgie by one arm and the man in the vest holds the other, as together they usher him out the door. The door whooshes shut behind him, catching Georgie by the tail end of his robe, making him think—for a second—that the store wanted him back, that it truly did value its customers.

But no, not even the store wants him, and Georgie trudges home, empty-handed, where he finds the message light on blinking, winking. A mile a minute. A mile a minute, it's blinking. He presses the message button, recoils in horror at the sound of Claudia's voice echoing in the empty house.

"Hey Georgie Porgie," she purrs. "I was just thinking about you. I was at this lecture? And it was sooo boring, all I could think of was getting back home, back to my snookums. My Georgie Porgie Pumpkin Eater."

Georgie wants her voice out of his head. He blinks, wondering if the torture was all in his mind and if really Claudia is still his—all his— and she really hadn't moved out and they really hadn't broken up and that she really is just at some sort of conference, and everything is as it was, as it should have been all along. Maybe.

(The man can dream, can't he?)

Georgie doesn't want to dream. He shakes his head, clearing his thoughts, realizing the message is old, from way back when. The real message plays:

"Hi Georgie," Claudia once again purrs. "Just wanted to check in. See what's going on. See how you've been doing. What you've got planned for the holidays."

Claudia's voice rises at the end of every sentence, or rather at the end of every word. Why has he never noticed before? Where has he been? And still Claudia's voice echoes in his head.

"I know how absent I've been," she says, "and how rough it's been, but Georgie, look at it from my perspective. It's just I needed to put 100% into my own family. You understand, don't you, Georgie? Don't you?"

Georgie reels. Who is this Claudia? This self-assured family woman, this woman Georgie's never met. Then . . . Then he remembers: Claudia was pregnant. She had the baby and raised it with her lesbian lover.

His baby. His sperm-child.

But then, yet another real message plays, and Georgie realizes that . . .

(Don't think about that.)

That Georgie, the one with the baby, must have been a different Georgie, that Claudia a different Claudia. As far as this Georgie is concerned—the real Georgie—none of that ever happened.

And so Georgie—the real Georgie—listens to the real message from Margaret, the real Margaret. The only Margaret.

"Hey, Georgie, it's me," she says quietly, sounding a little scared. "I just wanted to check in with you, see if you got in touch with your nanny yet. I think it's really important. I care about you a lot, you know . . . It's just . . . Well, anyway. Just go see her. That's all."

A pause for a moment. Nothing but silence. Dead silence. Then a fast goodbye and a click.

Georgie has not heard at all from Claudia. Only Margaret. Margaret, who says she cares for him. Margaret, who wants him to get better. Claudia never wanted him to get better. Claudia just wanted to hurt him . . . make him worse. She was happy to take his money and warp him into a twisted fuck. Georgie forgets that he's the one who asked her to, that he wanted to be sick, that healthy was just too hard, too dull. He forgets all that. He just thinks, with relief, of the possibility of that happy dream couple they could have been, if only he had applied himself.

Georgie digs frantically through his closet until he finds the jeans with that slip of paper in them with the nanny's address on it. He unfolds the paper, stares at the address in amazement. The house is close. Practically in his neighborhood.

What kind of sick fuck moves into the same neighborhood where his old nanny used to torture him? Then again, his parents bought him the house. Georgie looks out the door at the front lawn for a long moment then jogs sluggishly down the steps and across the grass.

Georgie climbs out of the town car; Ben shuts the door gently behind him as he takes his first steps. The house is a two-story, gray frame house with faded blue shutters that hang crookedly aside windows that are nearly opaque from years of accumulated grime and urban air. The small, front yard is practically a jungle, overgrown and out of control, salt grass brushes Georgie's knees and the hydrangea and pyracantha tower over his head. Dead ivy hangs limp and withered from the porch railing, and climbing honeysuckle peaks from the gutter. The sound of bees buzzing and leaves decomposing fill Georgie's ears, as he walks the overgrown path to the front porch.

He sees her, furiously rocking in a bentwood rocker and glaring at him.

"So you found me, finally?" she asks. Her voice is coarse as if she's spent her life smoking unfiltered Camels, and wisps of her cottony white hair blow around her face.

"Wha-what?" Georgie stammers, wondering how she knew, how she could have recognized him after these years.

"Through all that mess in my front yard," she says, pointing a skinny arm at the front lawn, and Georgie realizes he was wrong. She doesn't recognize him. She couldn't.

Still, he finds himself asking, "Do you remember me?"

He peers at her through the dark shadows of honeysuckle trees and dead vines. How could his nanny, that woman who had such power over him as a child, had made him tremble with terror, had pinched him, tormented him, swung him from his dick, how could she have become this scrawny, pathetic old woman? Was it the ultimate justice that she, who had once towered over him, now struggles to get to her feet out of that old, creaking chair, or just a cruel twist of fate?

Georgie briefly wonders what fate has in store for him, after all that he has done.

"Remember you?" the woman cackles again, harsh ancient air escaping from her lungs. "Who in this God damn world would bother to remember a pudgy little vermin like you?"

Georgie trembles, his foot pausing in mid-air on the first step.

"Aw, 'course I remember you, Georgie Gust," the woman cackles again. "I never forget a pretty face."

Georgie shudders, as he tries to remember what he's doing here. Is he supposed to confront this old woman? Beat her? Torment her—now that she's the weak one? Or beg her . . . for what? Forgiveness?

He looks at her again, as malevolent as Claudia but in a rocking chair. Maybe she's not so weak, after all. Age isn't everything.

"Yeah, well, I was uh . . ." Georgie clears his throat. "It's just that I wanted to see how you've been."

"Fine and dandy," she says, gesturing at the decay that surrounds her. "Livin' the dream."

Georgie walks up the steps, sits down uneasily on the empty rocker next to her. She grins at him, showing a mouth missing a myriad of teeth.

"Yeah," Georgie says, falling easily into the casual drawl of her speech. "Just thinkin' about the old days, you know. Used to have a lot of fun back then."

His throat threatens to constrict and choke him on the word "fun," but he gets it out anyway.

She smiles at him, a slight question in her eyes.

"Yeah, you used to spend hours and hours here," she says finally. "Sometimes it was hard to get you to go home."

"Yeah?" Georgie feels something twist in the pit of his stomach, like he is going to blow chunks. "Yeah?" he says again.

She nods sagely then stares at him from the corner of one eye as she chomps slowly on her gums.

"That's not what I remember," he spits out finally.

A wary look crosses her face.

Georgie continues, "What I remember is that you used to torture me."

She shakes her head vehemently back and forth, but he knows that she is lying.

"What I remember," he says, "is hating every minute here. I was miserable because of you."

The skinny old woman is still shaking her head—no no no.

Georgie is relentless. "You ruined everything for me," he screams at her. "Ev-everything. Every re-relationship I've ever had is ruined because of the w-way you . . ."

Then Georgie does something he rarely does, something he has not done since boarding school.

He bursts into tears.

In that vast nothingness, that horrible numbness deep inside me, there is a churning and gnashing, ripping out my insides, crushing my bones. My rib cage.

Everything shatters and falls apart. Everything gurgles up the back of my throat, drips from my mouth. Everything.

(Ben, is that you?)

And then.

Silence. Absolute dead silence.

As Georgie grows quiet, he feels a hard, bony hand resting on his knee. He remembers that hand, how it pinched and twisted at his balls, performed unspeakable acts on him.

The woman speaks—her voice seems young, now, almost human: "I'm sorry," she says.

Georgie hiccups.

"It was horrible," she says.

Georgie nods.

"Unspeakable," she whispers.

(But there are things that must be spoken . . . isn't that right, Ben? Ben?)

"But it wasn't all like that, you know," the woman says. Her eyes plead with him, like Claudia's. "What about your friend Marie? You two . . . You were like boyfriend and girlfriend when you were kids. So sweet to each other."

The woman's face breaks into a smile. Georgie can see that she's remembering better days. Sunny afternoons. Two kids in crisp, clean clothing running circles on the lawn, chasing after one another.

Georgie shakes his head, clearing his mind of the memory. "I don't remember that," he whispers. "Until last year, I didn't even remember you."

She grins wide. "Well, that's a blessing, isn't it?"

Georgie steps inside her rickety front door, feeling immediately ill at ease. The doorframe is crooked from years of warping from a sinking foundation; the floor rolls away beneath his feet, slightly downhill. It is dark and cool inside. Georgie waits a moment for his eyes to adjust.

"You see 'em?" the nanny's voice calls from the front porch. "They're right in there on the wall."

Georgie blinks and swivels around. An old sofa and sagging armchair rise out of the darkness, draped with gravity-warped afghan blankets and doilies, whose holes stretch like grinning mouths, their bottom lips drawn ever-closer to the floor.

Then he sees them. The pictures.

They line the wall beside the front door. Black-and-white, sepia toned—almost all of Georgie—so many of him that it goes beyond the nostalgic and slightly creepy to almost gruesome and nearly unbelievable.

(Do you believe it, Ben?

Ben?)

It's like Georgie was the only kid she ever babysat, or that he was the only one worth remembering.

And then there is the girl she mentioned—Marie. The wall is filled with pictures of her and Georgie posing in the bright sunlight, playing childish games. In one, he is lacing up her shoelaces. In another, she is riding him like a pony. The pictures flash in front of him, alternating between photo and memory . . . memory and photo.

He remembers her—the first Claudia. She stood before him in Keds and frilly pink dresses, stamping imperiously and ordering him about. Her moods were like storms across the ocean—quickly flashing in moments of terrifying manipulation, subsiding quickly once her wishes had been appeased.

He had been her slave—the first Georgie. Georgie Porgie, she'd called him. Before her, his name had been . . .

(Don't think about that, Georgie.

Ok.)

Looking at the pictures, Georgie realizes that this girl, this demanding, tiny, terrible woman, had taught him everything he knows. She was his first girlfriend, his model woman. She taught him how to love—the ups and downs of it, the grim, terrified clutching and the panicked, unreasonable, pushing away. She had taught him that love was pain and suffering . . . that it was better to hate the one you love, better to blame them for all the wretchedness they caused you.

I can do better than that, Georgie realizes suddenly. The fights, the torture—they do not have to happen. They don't have to be a part of me.

Georgie races from the house, his mind filled with the image of the happy American Dream lover he can be. He and Claudia and his son in his sunny and charming California bungalow, playing happy.

No. Being happy.

"Where you going so fast, puddin' pie?" the old woman drawls at his retreating back.

"Home," Georgie hollers, over his shoulder. "Home."

The woman cackles again, her mouth stretching into that impossible jack-o-lantern grin.

"Wouldn't be in such a hurry if I was you," she mutters. Her cackle follows Georgie all the way to the shining black limousine.

He climbs into the waiting limo and tells Ben, "Home, please."

Georgie is filled with an impossible delirium (just short of insanity). He knows he can be happy and perfect, if he just tries hard enough. He can make his own destiny. His mind rejoices. He can remake his own damn self any damn way he wants.

(Just like those new age books claim, eh Georgie-boy?)

Eh!

Ben pulls up in front of Georgie's house, tires screeching to a stop. Georgie leaps out of the car without waiting for Ben to open the door. He has no way of knowing, no reason to hope, but he knows that all his happiness is waiting for him inside. His happy dream future is only just steps away.

When Georgie flings open the door to his American Dream home, he runs headlong into a pitch-black room; thick smoke fills his nostrils, and something rough and scratchy encircles his neck. He is disoriented. Frightened. His fingers clutch at his neck, where he finds a rope—a noose actually, which is tightening around his throat. Georgie's fear escalates.

"Georgie," says her voice softly out of the darkness.

It is Claudia, his dream lover, his perfect woman. She will be nice to him if he tells her to be. She said she was tired of torturing him. She said so. He will pay her to be nice if that's what it takes. Georgie thinks dreamily of his future life as the noose tightens.

"Claudia?" he says.

Can't she see in his face that he doesn't want to play this game anymore? The rope is choking off his air supply. Georgie kicks and claws at his neck with his hands. He gurgles, trying to open his larynx to the air. He draws in a hissing stream of oxygen. Not enough. Then Georgie's mind overcomes his body's panic. She is not really killing him, after all. It is just one of those games that they are playing. She doesn't yet know that he is done with the torture game and wants to move on to something more blissful.

Ah, what the hell, Georgie thinks. One more time wouldn't hurt. For old time's sake. His gasping, bulbous, red-turned face grimaces that resembles a smile.

"What do you have to smile about?" Claudia demands from the darkness.

There is some movement on the rope as she ties it off. Then she steps into the small pool of light before him.

"What the fuck have you ever had to smile about, you freak?" she says.

Georgie finds his good humor starting to fade, as his face turns purple

"Do you see this?" She gestures to the circles beneath her eyes, her orange freckles.

"You," she says, "you did this to me. I never used to be this bad."

A sick, rattling moan escapes Georgie's lips. Spots dance before his eyes. He has heard all this before. When is she going to untie the rope? Is she going to bury him again, afterward? She stares at him in silence. For a moment, Georgie feels a stab of real fear run through him. Her eyes are haunted. Hollow. He can't see anything of the Claudia he remembers. Not in her eyes. Not in her face. The Claudia he remembers is gone.

Slowly, she smiles. Her curving lips fill his vision.

"I killed your son," Claudia whispers.

The words echo in Georgie's ears as if coming from a great distance.

"You didn't want him. You didn't care about him or about me. So I killed him."

She walks slowly to Georgie. He pulls desperately at the thick rope that rings his neck. He can't see past the fireworks exploding at the back of his eyes, but he can feel her. She touches his leg with her hand.

"I killed both of us," she whispers.

She yanks at the rope, cutting it deeper into his neck. She laughs.

"And now," she says, "I'm killing you."

Another tremendous pull and Georgie's world goes black. He can't hear her breathing. He can't feel her arms wrapped around him, or the rope around his neck.

He is nothing.

Finally. After all this time, he is nothing.

Dear Diary:

The best I can, to not create a catastrophe over anything.

Waking Up With Mr Clean

He wakes up in a world of white—a soft white glow. He tries to roll over but can't move his arms. For a moment he panics, jerking his arms frantically at his side. He can't breathe. A small cry escapes him. Then . . .

Then he understands the white room, and what it is that binds him, prevents his arms from moving.

It is a cell.

It is a straightjacket.

A man about Georgie's age taps on the small window in the door. Georgie looks up. The man smiles and opens the door.

"I see that you're up," the man says. He lifts a clipboard and props it on his forearm. "How are you doing today?"

"Wh-what?" Georgie says.

The man squints at him.

"Do you know where you are?" he asks.

Georgie shakes his head.

The man inhales deeply. "Mercyhurst Hospital?" he says. "Remember now?"

Georgie shakes his head 'no.'

"You remember me?"

Again, Georgie shakes his head.

"Dr Weinstein?" the man says. "Your psychiatrist?"

Georgie tries to shake the cobwebs from his head. "So I'm uh . . . I'm uh . . . I'm not dead?"

Dr Weinstein looks at him with a slight smile. "Alive as ever," he says. Georgie detects a slightly ironic tone, but doesn't understand it. He decides that it's nothing.

"Where's Claudia?" Georgie demands.

"Who?"

"Claudia. My girlfriend."

Dr Weinstein frowns slightly, notes something on his iPad then glances at Georgie.

"Who's Claudia?" he says.

"I told you, my girlfriend."

"You have no girlfriend."

"Red hair. Freckles," Georgie says.

"There's no one like that. Not here. And there's no Claudia."

Georgie stares at his doctor and then, as a smile spreads across Georgie's face, his arms, his neck, his entire body relaxes. No Claudia. She never existed, never hurt him. Never killed him. He breathes a sigh of relief.

And yet, at the same time . . . If she didn't exist, then . . . Then the pain of her nonexistence is almost stronger than the pain of her actual existence. If she wasn't real, then what else wasn't—*isn't*—real? No, he decides, somewhere Claudia does exist, somewhere the doctor can't find, but no—Claudia was too real not to have existed at all.

The doctor is wrong.

And then, as if the doctor can read Georgie's mind, he asks, "Do you know how long you've been here? At Mercyhurst?"

Georgie shakes his head. He doesn't want to know.

"Fifteen years," the doctor says. "Nearly half your life."

Georgie reels back, struggling to free his arms. The doctor notices.

"The trick to getting out of those," he says, motioning to the restraints, "is to stop fighting them. Stop fighting us."

Georgie's mind is blank. He can't remember fighting anyone. Ever. He is complacent, isn't he? Acquiescent. He doesn't fight.

"Do you remember what you're doing here?"

Again, Georgie's mind is blank.

"I don't mean at Mercyhurst. I mean here . . . ." This time, the doctor gestures around the room, at the cushioned walls, the small barred window. "Do you remember what you did to end up in seclusion? To end up in restraints?"

Georgie's eyes widen; he shakes his head frantically back and forth. All he can remember is Claudia. Margaret. The house in the woods. The pain. That's what he remembers.

"Well," the doctor says, turning to leave. "Why don't we give you some time to think? I'm sure once your mind clears, you'll remember."

And then the doctor, pulling a jangling ring of keys from his pocket, unlocks the door and walks out, leaving Georgie completely alone, restrained, and still unable to remember a thing.

The doctor sticks his head in the door: "It's not that bad. Really. Mercyhurst is state of the art."

State of the art, but it's still fifteen years. Fifteen years of a life only imagined. He stumbles, falls to his knees. Claudia. Margaret. A dream. A dream. A dream . . . Something wets his cheeks, rolls to his chin.

Tears. Georgie is crying.

He sobs, feeling the loss and the terror rise up in him. Then it subsides. Leaving him empty. Clean. Some time passes as Georgie tries desperately to comprehend a situation that seems impossible.

Georgie gasps, pulling at his restraints, staring at the ceiling above. His personal hell. This can't be happening. This can't be real. It comes to him, then. It isn't real. This—Mercyhurst, the restraints—this is the dream. The hallucination.

He screams into the silent room: "Somebody help me. Somebody. Claudia?"

He knows she won't come.

He tries again: "I demand that all my angels, spirit guides, all of you who know me, who want to help. I demand: Touch my head so I know you're here. Wake me up from this nightmare."

Nothing happens, and once again Georgie sobs. But then . . .

He feels a hand on his head. He moves his head, trying to look, trying to see. And then Ben's face comes into view, smiling at him. Smiling at Georgie.

"You?"

Ben nods slowly.

"I can see you," Georgie says.

"Yes," Ben says.

Or is it the voice—the voice in Georgie's head—the voice that's been there always, ever since. (*Don't think about that.*)

He stares closely into Ben's face, taking in the nose, the mouth, the cheeks. "You're not bad-looking," Georgie says. "You have the face I should have had. The face I always wanted."

Ben smiles as if Georgie's said something funny. Something clever.

And then Georgie looks deeply into Ben's eyes, a mirror of the soul. His soul.

(*It's impossible to say. Neither of us turned out quite the way we thought we would.*)

"Why can I see you now?"

(*Couldn't you see me before?*)

"I don't know."

(*You don't have to talk, you know. You can just think.*)

"You're always listening, aren't you?"

(*Yup.*)

Georgie relaxes, staring at the blank, acoustic ceiling, thinking nothing, wanting nothing. Somewhere, even if he can't see him, somewhere Ben waits. Ben is there. Ben has always been there, always will be.

"Are we dead?" Georgie asks.

Ben gives a mental shrug. *(How should I know?)*

"You're not good for much, are you?"

(Fuck you.)

Georgie longs to pick at his fingernails, but his arms are still tightly restrained. He can't even scratch himself. He can do nothing but stare at the ceiling, turn his head and stare at a wall.

"Who are you?" Georgie finally asks. Ahhh. The million-dollar question.

(You, Georgie. I'm you. Just as you, in all your delusions, your hallucinations are me. We are one.)

Georgie wants to jump free, slam himself into the wall, but, even if could, what would be the point? What would he gain? Instead . . .

"Why is my driver named Ben?" he asks.

(Why is your driver named Ben? Or why I am your driver?)

Ben seems to be laughing. *(You never listen, do you? Dr C explained it to you hundreds of times. I drive. You ride. Simple as that. Or some such bullshite.)*

"I don't get it."

(Bullshite. I drive, but you tell me where, when. You're more than the rider, the passenger. Aren't you?)

Georgie wants to rub his eyes, clear his head. "Huh?"

(I'm not your alter ego, Georgie; you're mine.)

Georgie's mind whirls. He doesn't understand.

(You're not real. You've never been real.)

Georgie nods. Of course. That's it. He's not real. He's not the driver, not the rider. Not the passenger. He's never really been here. Not in Mercyhurst. Not with Claudia. It is a blessing. A relief.

Georgie closes his eyes, sinks slowly away. Now. Now he gets it. Farther and farther he sinks. The room fades. Ben fades. Life fades. Somewhere—far, far off in the distance—Georgie hears Ben's voice screaming:

"I want a cigarette, goddamnit. Somebody in this fucking shitehole bring me a goddamn cigarette. Did you hear me? I'm Ben Schreiber, and I want a goddamn fucking cigarette. And I want it now."

Georgie hears the voice. He smiles.

Dear Diary:

The best I can, to not overreact, no matter what. Yikes.

If you think about it, the whole world, at least my miniature world, is encompassed within the universe, this universe that we can only imagine as seemingly having no end. So with the death of Claudia, going back in time to the beginning, you can even trace the speed of light, it's an incredible phenomenon. People wondered how the damn thing was created in the first place. Back in the year 1000, men never lived long enough nor did Claudia, and they didn't travel far enough to get really beyond the town where they lived, so they could only imagine what existed beyond the hills and it's ironic because the things that existed right in front of them, they knew extremely well, every tree, every villa, every knoll of land. But they could only image what existed beyond that, and one doesn't know, we fear, ultimately. So beyond the hills, and beyond that dense primeval forest, existed fairies and sometimes demons that would rush out and destroy them, or fierce indescribable animals that would tear them apart if they ever wandered beyond their clod fields. Reality is strange. And so, I allowed Claudia to decide my imagination . . . my reality. It all began on the road.

The Story Continues

Made in the USA
San Bernardino, CA
26 February 2019